# CYBORG HUNTER
*Kill or Be Killed*

by

Neale Rawlings

*Hardwood Pond Publishing*
*Minnesota*

First Edition

Cover design by Neale Rawlings
Printed in the United States of America
ISBN (Paperback): 979-8-9937763-0-9
ISBN (eBook): 979-8-9937763-1-6

# Dedication

This book is dedicated to my loving family.

I started it with a simple idea—to help my young son get interested in reading. The books at school felt boring and uninspiring for a kid with a big imagination, so we sat down together and began writing a few chapters of a story I'd been thinking about.

It worked. He became excited about reading, then moved on to graphic novels and fantasy adventures. Today, he's an avid reader as a young man. Mission accomplished.

The book itself never really left that unfinished stage until now. He kept rereading what we had written and loved it. In fact, some of those early chapters remain nearly untouched because of that affection. That's part of what makes this story special.

I hope you enjoy it as much as I did creating it.

# TABLE OF CONTENTS

# TABLE OF CONTENTS (continued)

*"When the rules are written by machines,
humanity becomes the glitch."*
—*System Audit Report, Cipher Division*

# Chapter 1—The Rush

Nick ran through the mall. He knew he only had fifteen more minutes until time expired; he needed to find his way out to the parking lot, get into his car, and drive as fast as he could. The cyborg had processed Nick's every possible move out of the mall, like a chess player determining all the next possible combinations of moves. It also knew it only a short time left to kill Nick, as it was programmed to do.

Nick slipped into the nearest department store and made his way through the men's clothing area.

"Can I help you?" asked a salesclerk.

He muttered, "No thank—" Before he finished his sentence, he remembered the cyborg had voice recognition software and could pick up his voice from nearly anywhere. "Dammit!" he knocked over the shoe display as he quickly made his way to the nearest exit.

The cyborg quickly picked up Nick's location and headed to the department store.

"Watch where you're going, mister," said a teenage boy as the cyborg bumped him, but it was on a mission to locate Nick, not to argue with punks. However, it was getting thirsty for an Orange Julius.

"Seven more minutes," thought Nick. He was also having the rush of his life. He had always been a highly successful video gamer, and when he had the opportunity to play the ultimate video game, *Cyborg Hunter*, he jumped at it.

Ten K to play and have a Level 1, 2, or 3 cyborg hunt you for twenty-four hours. Lose and you're dead—it played for keeps. Live and you're out the ten K, but at least you are alive. Destroy the cyborg before it kills you, and you get your money back.

He thought, not yet. I've made it twenty-three-plus hours; I'm not giving up now.

He was also thankful it was only a Level 1 cyborg, as he knew he would probably be dead by now otherwise.

Back in Mission Control, the creators were hoping for another cyborg victory. As gruesome as it may seem, death was good for business. Dead clients meant this game had proven to be the ultimate thrill and was to be taken seriously.

With so many things being conquered and thrills and rushes harder to find, people had seen this as the opportunity to feel more alive, even if it meant certain death.

Level 1 was a starting point for most; it was a sophisticated half-machine with many capabilities— GPS, infrared and night vision, voice recognition, and Logica CMG facial recognition, for starters.

A Level 3 was near suicide to the inexperienced, and even to some of the more seasoned players. It had highly sophisticated tracking capabilities and was linked to satellite and computer databases worldwide. If you made a purchase with your credit card at any store anywhere, it would instantly get that information and could then link to live satellite and track your movements from there. If your image were captured by a security camera, it would receive that information instantly as well.

All cyborgs were programmed with the intimate details of their opponent. The differences from Levels 1 to 3 were minor but significant—speed of learning, data processing, level of smart A.I., weapon accuracy, and intensity of pursuit were all set to the maximum at Level 3.

The weapon of choice for most cyborgs was a standard-issue semi-automatic twelve-gauge shotgun. They had a multitude of weapons at their disposal, including but not limited to RPGs, sniper rifles, chain guns, machine guns, and swords. Weapon choice depended on the profile of who the cyborg was hunting and personal preference. A stronger, heavily armed, and more experienced foe meant more and better artillery.

Those who were not intelligent enough or didn't understand the seriousness of the game were easy prey for the cyborg. A simple handgun, a twelve-gauge blast to the face, a stabbing, or even an '80s-style beating would suffice in eliminating most people. The intelligent and more experienced players, however, had studied and knew what the cyborgs were capable of, having learned their weaknesses before they even began to play. It was a matter of life or death.

Out in the parking lot, Nick now knew that the cyborg was aware of his general position. He decided his car would be the first place the cyborg would go, so he stayed on foot. Staying low and moving quickly but quietly, he headed toward the bus stop across the street. With some luck, a bus would come right away, and he could sneak on undetected and make a safe and timely getaway.

The cyborg ran out the nearest exit and quickly scanned the parking lot for Nick's vehicle. It didn't take long to find it. It walked toward the vehicle and was prepared to blow Nick's head off. He wasn't there, and time was running low.

"Hey, are you one of those Cyborg Hunters?" asked an older man.

The cyborg looked coldly at him.

"I saw a guy creeping around those vehicles across the parking lot," he said as he pointed toward the southern end of the lot. "Maybe that's your guy."

The cyborg turned and headed toward the bus stop.

Nick waited for a moment at the bus stop. While the final few minutes were winding down, he still wasn't feeling comfortable. He reached into his pocket to remove the only weapon he had on him—an electrical circuit jammer. If he were to get close enough to the cyborg without being killed and attach it magnetically, it would jam the circuits and shut it down. He was hoping to avoid a confrontation, especially in the last three minutes, but he still needed to be prepared.

A bus approached, and Nick was eager to get on it. Looking north, he noticed an ominous-looking figure walking his way—the cyborg, he thought. It was still over a hundred yards out and scanning the parking lot for him. He tried ducking behind the bus shelter to wait for the approaching bus; the cyborg caught the movement, recognized him, and started to move in.

Nick saw it lock in on his location and could almost taste his heart beating—it was so far up into his throat. "This is it—kill or be killed," he said to himself.

Nick started playing video games as a young boy. He mastered nearly every game he played in very short order. When he got a little older, he began playing competitively, and by the age of twenty-four had earned nearly six hundred thousand dollars in tournaments worldwide. As he approached twenty-six, video games had lost their luster. It was a large amount of time to dedicate, and he was tired of sitting inside for days on end playing the same games over and over so he could master them. A lack of a social life was also wearing on him. He wanted a wife and a family of his own one day, so he had to start living out of the shadows. Those wasted years had also left him yearning to experience something more—he wanted to do something exciting, something that would make him feel more alive—and he wanted to do it before he committed to starting a new life for himself.

He had been intrigued with the idea of the game *Cyborg Hunter* for a few years now.

Dr. Madeline Jones began working with cyborgs to help people—helping the elderly, teaching kids, walking dogs, and whatever someone needed help with. Cyborgs were generally better than robots because they were part human and could make a connection in a way a robot could not—human brain power with robotic durability and strength.

Dr. Madeline Jones developed a way to create lab-grown brains, program them, and use them in her cyborgs. However, funding from the government eventually dried up because of the ethics of using these; they were, after all, human in a way, and this was perceived as wrong. Private funding quickly followed suit.

With nowhere to turn and cyborgs to use, Dr. Madeline Jones decided to create the game *Cyborg Hunter*—a live-action video game like no other. Sure, there was AR and VR, but people were getting bored; even with realism, something was missing. Actual cyborgs hunting you down for a real game of life and death was the next level. People paid big money for the ultimate experience. Sure, there was a good chance they would be killed, but for that twenty-four hours they really lived. It was a huge success, and people played all over the world.

Nick had heard stories of people being killed by their particular hunter, and he paid special attention to how players spent their final hours or how they overcame the odds and were victorious. He learned that many of the losers would try to hide, hunker down, and outlast the cyborg for those twenty-four hours. This was always a fatal error. These cyborgs knew everything about you—family members and their addresses, workplaces, shopping habits, the cars driven by everyone, credit-card info, etc. They had all the information they needed to quickly find, track, and kill you. There was no hiding.

The next deadly error was confrontation—trying to fight the cyborg one-on-one. A cyborg would learn as it went and become even stronger and smarter the longer the fight wore on. If you didn't defeat it immediately, it would quickly learn your capabilities and weaknesses and begin to anticipate your moves until you were defeated. Victory and intelligence went hand in hand. Constant awareness of your surroundings, staying undetected and on the move, and diligent preparation were all necessary to survive.

Nick had trained and prepared for nearly six months before taking on his cyborg. Up to this point, it had been everything he hoped for—exciting, competitive, and an adrenaline rush like he had never experienced before. However, this was the closest the cyborg had gotten to killing him, and while exciting, reality has a way of turning that excitement into terror. Nick had to regain his edge and last a couple more minutes—the longest minutes of his life.

The bus pulled up, and Nick quickly got on; luckily, he was the only one waiting. The door closed, and the bus pulled away as he grabbed a seat. The cyborg rushed to reach the bus and managed to grab hold of the side door. The other passengers moved away from the area, as they knew what was coming and wondered who the poor bastard was that this cyborg was after. The cyborg managed to open the door and enter the moving bus.

Nick turned to look at the approaching cyborg and took what little shelter he had behind his seat as the cyborg readied its twelve-gauge sawed-off shotgun. It needed to fire at extremely close range and was programmed not to harm anyone except its primary target. If it needed to kill Nick by choking him out, it would do so if it meant not harming anyone else nearby.

Mission Control had begun watching this particular event unfold from an installed camera on the cyborg in the last five minutes. They huddled around a single large monitor hoping for a kill.

"Since it's on a bus and in the public's eye, I hope it doesn't blow the guy's head off with the shotgun," said Dr. Madeline Jones. "That would be awfully messy and would look awfully bad."

"Yeah, hopefully it can just choke the son-of-a—" The audio feed spiked, cutting him off.

"Anyway a kill is a kill."

The bus came to a stop at a light, and Nick jumped at the opportunity. Diving forward and grabbing the lever to open the door, he made a run for it. The cyborg ran to the open door, and seeing it had a clear shot, fired a round at Nick from the twelve-gauge. The spread was way too wide to hit Nick at that distance, except for a few bits of shot that caught him in the backs of his legs. It burned, but it didn't slow him down. He ran, knowing time was about to expire—and he survived.
The cyborg went into default mode, grabbed a seat on the bus, and it was over.

# Chapter 2—The Aftermath

The street outside the bus depot was empty and wet, the kind of night that left a taste of metal on the tongue. Nick limped along the curb with his hand pressed to his side, the adrenaline finally leaking out of him like heat from a cracked engine. He could still feel the echo of the shotgun blast in his legs. It burned, but he was upright. He was breathing. He was alive.

"Twenty-four hours, one cyborg, and I feel more alive than I ever did behind a keyboard," he said to no one. It sounded ridiculous in the dark, but true things often did.

A siren drifted somewhere far off. He stopped beneath a streetlight, checked the torn fabric, and kept walking. The rush had been a tidal wave. Now there was the undertow—shaking hands, a hollow chest, and a brain that would not stop replaying the last five minutes frame by frame.

Across town, the arena's mission room settled into the hush that followed any completed match. Screens bled to gray. Chairs scraped. Techs signed off with soft, practiced voices, stacking clipboards, powering down. Only one monitor still held an image—Nick caught mid-stride on a bus aisle, eyes fixed on the thing that had come to end him. The time stamp blinked at the corner. Someone had left the sound off.

Dr. Madeline Jones watched the quiet picture, chin in her palm. A single desk lamp left a halo on the surface beside her. The telemetry graph scrolled in clean lines: pulse spikes, cortisol surges, micro-tremors in the hands. Fear, will, fear, will. In the combined curve she saw a pattern she knew well.

"Fear as the trigger," she murmured, almost tenderly. "Courage as the cure."

An assistant hovered at the door, hesitant to disturb her. "Do you want me to close the Kade file for the night, Doctor?"

"Archive it under behavioral optimization," she said without looking away. "Tag the final five minutes."

The door clicked shut. She rewound the footage. When Nick reached for the bus lever, she paused and studied his face. Not the bravado of a man who thought he could not die. The clarity of a man who chose not to. There was a difference.

Nick made it home on the steady autopilot of habit. He washed the grit off his skin and the blood out of the shirt, hissing once when the hot water hit the peppering in his calves. He taped what needed taping and found he could finally unclench his jaw. The apartment was as he'd left it—one plant that refused to die, a window that stuck if you opened it too far, trophies lined up on a narrow shelf like polite ghosts. A cheap metal cup from a regional tournament. A photo with a sponsor backdrop and a grin that belonged to a younger man who hadn't learned yet what winning cost.

He sat with the cup in his hands and let the weight of it settle. He had lived whole years in rooms like this, lit by screens, trying to squeeze meaning out of simulation. Somewhere along the line, the prize had turned to noise. Tonight had been different. The stakes were not a bracket and a check. They were skin, tendon and air.

He thumbed his wrist console and brought up the official match reel, the one every player could request after their time was up. He watched the last ten minutes again, but this time as a student and not a survivor. The cyborg had taken a bad angle at the first exit—too direct, expecting him to run a straight line. It had corrected immediately. That micro-delay had been the window. There were other tells, too. It favored the left on quick pivots. There was a four-second logic loop between visual reacquisition and trigger squeeze when bystanders were present, even with a clear shot. He had felt that delay without thinking. He had always been good at feeling where code would go next.

"Every bot has a tell," he said, setting the cup back on the shelf. "Even the real ones."

A thump rattled the mail slot. He blinked at the hour and crossed to the door. A flat black envelope waited on the mat with no return address. Inside, a card lay in tight foam—a matte rectangle with a small, raised sigil and a line of text debossed so faint you had to angle it toward the window to read it.

ADVANCE TIER CLEARANCE AUTHORIZED
CONTACT WITHIN 72 HOURS

He held it a long time, thumb tracing the edge. The old reflex, the one that smelled like competition and sounded like a crowd, rose in his throat. He swallowed it down and set the card on the table.

He tried to sleep and simply couldn't. At some point near dawn he gave up and walked. The city was a softer thing at that hour, all washed concrete and yellow light. Delivery trucks shouldered through puddles. A baker propped open a door and let a rope of warm air spill onto the sidewalk, smelling of butter and clean heat. A street screen replayed the highlight reel with a voice-over designed to make the game run seem noble.

Someone on a bench watched and said, "Guy got lucky," and someone else said, "Nah, he trained."

Nick studied the reflections in the glass—an overlay of his face with his feet moving beneath him, with the looping advertisement for the game in the corner promising the one thing a modern man could not buy anywhere else: feeling. *Live once. Die right.*

He passed a church with its doors open for morning prayer. The inside was small and quiet, a rectangle of wood and patience. He did not go in. He stood at the threshold and felt something like grief and something like relief and then kept walking. A thought came in and sat down without asking: we used to make places where the heart could rest. Now we make machines to frighten it back into beating.

The world wasn't colder now—just quieter in a way that felt wrong. Like a note had gone missing from the chord everyone else still swore they could hear.

At three a.m., Dr. Madeline Jones finally left the mission room and climbed the narrow stairs to the lab above. The glass walls were clean enough to double as a second night outside; she could see the first hint of morning like a rumor over the city's edge. She keyed her recorder out of habit. Words came more easily that way, laid out in sequence and judged later.

"Subject Kade exhibits rapid threat recognition and adaptive behavior under acute pressure," she said in that low, precise voice that fit her hands. "The pattern is not unique, but it is efficient. If we can replicate the response pathway without the surrounding damage, we have a model for eliminating trauma triggers in controlled populations. Fear can be shortened. Pain can be managed. Purpose can be taught."

She stopped, not because she doubted the sentence, but because she could hear what it might sound like to someone who didn't know the data. She crossed to the window and leaned one palm against the cool, perfect pane. Somewhere below, a janitor turned a buffer down an empty hallway. Somewhere above, day was gathering itself.

She did care. That was the part some of them never understood, the ones who only saw the weapons drills and the spreadsheets. Caring had been the mistake, she supposed, for people who wanted a quiet life. She had not been given that sort of life.

She switched off the recorder. It did not need to hear her say the rest out loud.

By seven the sky had gone the color of wet paper. Nick stood outside a diner and watched the cook flip eggs on a steel surface until they were exactly right. He went

16

in, sat at the counter, and ate the kind of plate that forgives you—coffee, salt, something that had once been alive and was still generous enough to be good to you. When he paid, he realized he was smiling.

Back in the apartment, the black card still waited on the entry table where he had left it. He tucked it into a drawer, not as refusal, not as acceptance, but as a way to remind himself that he could still choose the hour and the terms.

The room was busy with the small, practical noises of morning. Pipes talking. A neighbor's television heard through the wall. Shoes drying by the heater. He picked up the controller on the shelf, turned it over in his hands, and put it back. The trophies watched him without opinion.

He was tired so he decided to lie down on the couch. Just before sleep found him, the thought returned, softer now, less boast than promise: maybe next time it wouldn't be about proving anything to anyone. Maybe it would be about finding out who he was when the game stripped the rest away.

Across the city, Dr. Madeline Jones stood at the high window and watched the first full band of light break over the buildings. "One step closer," she said.

# Chapter 3—The Rooftop

The observation lab was nearly dark. Only the soft blue light of monitors moved across Dr. Madeline Jones's face. The data from Nick Kade's hunt replayed in looping graphs—heart-rate spikes, cortisol surges, fear peaking just before clarity. She watched it the way others might study a symphony, tracing the patterns with the tip of one finger.

"He faced extinction and adapted in seconds," she said quietly. "That's not instinct. That's learning."

Her assistant hovered near the door. "The next trial is prepped, Doctor. Specter Unit online."

Madeline adjusted her glasses, eyes still on the display. "Increase environmental stress, more altitude, open exposure. I want to see how long cognition holds when there's nowhere to hide."

"Keep safety protocols active?"

A small pause. "Yes," she said, "for now."

She watched the rain slide down the observation glass and thought, not for the first time, that fear was the truest constant in evolution. Every species had been sculpted by it, yet humanity spent lifetimes trying to erase it. Perhaps that was the problem, she thought. Perhaps progress was meant to frighten us.

She turned to a new monitor. Rain swept across a rooftop camera. "Commence Trial Twelve."

Destiny sprinted across the rain-slick roof, breath sharp in the cold. Sixteen stories up, a city of light stretched beneath her, reflections sliding off glass towers like oil. Somewhere behind her, the air shimmered. That meant Specter was close.

She'd studied footage: its camouflage flickered when wet. Good, tonight everything was wet.

She vaulted an air duct, dropped to a crouch, eyes scanning for distortion.

The rain was cold enough to sting, turning the rooftop into a mirror of light and motion. Her breath came in short bursts that fogged and vanished. She could smell the city, the copper bite of ozone, exhaust, and the faint sweetness of wet concrete after heat. Every sound felt amplified, sharpened: the creak of metal, the buzz of a dying sign. Her body had become an antenna for survival.

A voice in her earpiece crackled: "Four minutes remaining, player. Heart rate 136. Keep it down."

She tore the earpiece out. The voices were worse than the silence.

Destiny ducked behind a vent. She knew the trick was to make it hunt something else. She drew her knife and sliced her palm, warm blood against the metal. Then she flung her jacket, soaked red, toward the edge.

A blur snapped toward it, a faint distortion, a whisper of hydraulics, and Destiny saw her opening. She charged.

The two collided near the ledge, the camouflage rippling like water peeling from glass. Specter's hand clamped her throat; servos whined.

"You have one minute remaining," it said in a calm male voice.

Destiny jammed her bleeding hand against its visor. The optical feed splashed with bio-data noise, her blood became static in its system. Then she used her other hand to slam the emergency flare into its chest.

Light exploded between them, crimson magnesium.

Specter reeled back, camo failing completely. For the first time, she saw its face, smooth metal, no eyes, only reflection.

Specter steadied, recalibrated, and mimicked Destiny's own heartbeat through its speaker, a perfect echo.

"You wanted to feel alive," it said, her own voice played back to her.

Destiny laughed, half hysteria, half defiance, and kicked the flare deeper into its chest cavity. The flare detonated.

Specter staggered backward, flames licking through armor.

"Zero minutes," it said, then toppled over the edge.

Destiny collapsed on the roof, exhausted.

Rain pinged on metal far below. The city lights flickered, one by one, until only the red flare burned in the night.

She stayed there, kneeling, the rain cooling her skin until she shivered. The flare's glow painted the rooftop in waves of red that pulsed like a heartbeat. Her pulse answered it, slow now, deliberate. For the first time in hours, she remembered she had one. Somewhere far below, sirens began to rise, late and distant, human. Destiny wiped her hand across her mouth, tasting salt and metal, and whispered to the night, "I win."

In the lab, the monitors went white for a moment before resolving into still frames, the flare's ignition frozen mid-burst, the edges of the roof melting into static.

"Trial Twelve complete," her assistant said. "Player alive. Cyborg terminated."

Madeline sat back, hands folded. "Good, survival under extreme stress re-wires the brain. It leaves stronger pathways."

She opened two data files: one labeled *Kade, N.* and the other *Voss, D.* Two graphs appeared, different people, different fights, but the patterns matched almost perfectly.

Her assistant frowned. "That can't be right. Different conditions, separate sessions—"

Madeline zoomed in, overlaying the lines until they formed a single rhythm. "Fear isn't the problem," she said softly. "It's the doorway."

"Do you want to schedule another trial?"

"Yes, and double the neural feedback. Let's see what happens when they feel what the machine feels."

"That could push the bio-sync past safe limits."

Madeline smiled faintly, eyes still fixed on the screen. "Then we'll learn how much safety is worth."

The assistant left, footsteps fading. Alone, Madeline replayed the moment of ignition frame by frame, pausing where the flare's light met the cyborg's face. For half a second before collapse, the machine's reflection seemed almost human, eyes where there should have been none. She stared at it until the image dissolved into white noise and said softly, "Almost there."

Madeline turned off the monitor. "Send a retrieval team," she said quietly. "Let's see what Specter learned before it died."

Rain ticked against the lab's tall windows, a thin sound like static. On the monitor, the two graphs pulsed together, human and machine in perfect time. Madeline reached out, touched the point where they overlapped, and for a moment she imagined she could feel the heartbeat through the glass.

# Chapter 4—The Healing Initiative

They called it a review, not a demonstration. The invitation said **Closed-Door Neuro-Symbiosis Review** and listed the start time in twenty-four–hour format, the kind of detail that made people feel official. The security gate took retinal scans and a palm print. The elevator required a second pass and descended so smoothly it might have been falling. No press. No cameras beyond the lab's own. Inside, men and women who never blinked at budget lines stood with their hands folded, trying to look like they weren't excited.

Dr. Madeline Jones stood in front of a long window that looked onto the procedure bay. She wore no lab coat this time, just a dark dress and a thin chain at her collarbone that caught the white light when she moved. On the other side of the glass, a man in his thirties lay on a table, eyes closed, scalp partially shaved to show the neat curve of the implant halo beneath the skin. On the clipboard he was Subject T-41, but on the intake form he had written his name carefully, each letter upright and plain. Years of teaching himself to write from a chair had made him careful with small tasks.

"Ladies and gentlemen," Madeline said, her voice soft enough that people leaned in. "You will see gait initiation and standing stability today. No exoskeleton. No tether."

The military liaison at the end of the row cleared his throat as if to show he had one. The investor beside him kept his face polite, the way rich men do when they don't want to look like they're hoping.

Madeline nodded to the tech in the bay. The tech touched the tablet. The subject's eyes fluttered, opened. He stared at the ceiling until someone said his name. He turned his head, saw Madeline through the glass, and smiled politely. He was used to being looked at.

"Take your time," Madeline said into the intercom. "There's no rush."

He flexed his fingers. The system mapped the movement—clean, symmetric signals. On the far wall, four lines began to dance: musculoskeletal output, cortical drive, autonomic balance, artifact suppression. The liaison watched the lines like weather. The investor watched Madeline.

"Breathe," she said, more to the graphs than to the man. "Feel your feet."

His left hand found the rail. He curled his fingers around it and pulled, then eased off as the first tremor shivered through his core. The tremor subsided. He brought his right hand over, mirrored the grip. He did not ask if he could. He did not ask if he should. He had been asked those questions enough.

The lift happened almost by accident, a thinking-with-the-body that startled him. He was not standing—he was rising, and the difference mattered. His feet flattened. His knees quivered and caught. He let out a sound that was neither laugh nor sob, and then he was simply there, higher than he had been in years, the world different by four feet.

No one clapped. It would have been obscene in that room. An exhale moved through the observers like a low wind. The liaison's jaw shifted, working through a thought he didn't want to show. The investor's eyes shone the way mirrors do.

"Walk when you like," Madeline said.

The first step was slow and cautious because dignity always is. He lifted, placed, shifted weight, repeated. Three steps. Four. The tremor came back and slid off him. He looked down at his legs as if they were strangers.

On the screen, the four lines arranged themselves into something that looked familiar to Madeline. The autonomic balance curve rose at the same beat as cortical drive. She touched the glass, fingertip against the pane, not to be dramatic but because she wanted a second contact point with the moment.

The subject reached the end of the rail and turned with effort. His eyes met hers. Something about the focus was wrong, not vacant, not dull, exactly, but as if the light reached the surface and found no purchase. A sheen without depth. It lasted a breath and was gone.

"Thank you," he said to the world in general. His voice shook in the middle and then steadied. "Thank you."

"You're doing it," Madeline said. "We're just helping."

The liaison leaned toward the investor. "If she can do this reliably, rehab costs implode."

"Rehab becomes investment," the investor murmured. "Imagine licensing."

Madeline heard both and neither. She watched the four lines and the fifth window in her head. Specter's final telemetry had looked like this in the last twenty-seconds, the human pulse braided with machine calm until the pattern became something else. She had stayed up two nights isolating the segment and building the model that translated it into a safe human threshold. Safe enough, she corrected herself. There are no safe thresholds, only ones we agree to call that.

The subject took another step. His right foot dragged a fraction. The artifact-suppression line blipped. The tech adjusted. The foot placed. The world continued.

"Record all intervals," Madeline said, not into the intercom but to the room. "We'll need time points for longitudinal analysis. Pre and post."

The liaison straightened. "Post?"

"I'm not interested in parlor tricks," Madeline said, as if explaining it for the first time to herself. "A trick is a moment. I'm interested in permanence."

When it was over, and the subject was seated again with blankets tucked around his knees, the room began to breathe normally. People drifted toward the small table with bottled water and the plate of cookies that appeared out of nowhere. Someone shook Madeline's hand and said historic. Someone else said game-changer and meant market share, not mercy. The liaison asked for a briefing memo with no adjectives in it. Madeline nodded to all of them and kept her gaze on the glass.

Through it, she saw the subject run a hand across his thighs as if memorizing the shape. The wrongness in his eyes flickered again and passed. She filed it away, not as dismissal but as something to solve.

The observers left as they had entered, in a hush that was not reverence but the calculation people use when deciding what to want next. The elevator took them away. The room reassembled itself into equipment and lists. The techs went back to being people who had to pee or call a sitter.

Only Madeline remained by the window when the bay lights dimmed to night mode. In the reflection on the glass, her face hovered beside the floating graphs, as if she were already half data. She rested her forehead against the cool pane. It smelled faintly of cleaner and a trace of the coffee someone had set too near it earlier.

Her console chimed. **Specter Core Archive 12-A: Sync Complete.** The file hung in the corner of the screen like a note she had left herself and kept avoiding.

She opened it. The room changed with the color of the display.

There was no video—most of the cycles were cooked in the rooftop fall and the flare's heat—but the neural telemetry had survived in pieces. She spliced it the way she had learned to splice music in college for a boy who played guitar badly. The sequence rebuilt itself: rising pulse, matched logic, the overlay like two hands finding each other.

She replayed the segment she had isolated, the point where fear and clarity climbed the same stair. On another window, she brought up T-41's standing sequence. She matched the beats. She watched the two windows pulse in time, felt the old thrill that had nothing to do with power and everything to do with the right answer finally showing itself.

Her assistant stepped into the lab quietly, because some moments should be approached that way.

"Doctor," he said, keeping his voice small. "The patient's vitals are steady. But the blink reflex is… delayed. He doesn't respond to the light test as quickly as baseline."

Madeline did not turn her head. "How delayed?"

"Point eight seconds on average. One point three at longest."

"Artifact suppression," she said. "The system is still cleaning noise. It will normalize."

He nodded, not reassured but unwilling to argue with a woman who watched graphs like constellations and had just lifted a man back into his life.

"There's something else," he said. "During the standing interval, the heart rate syncs perfectly to the algorithm. It isn't just following—it's—"

"Leading," Madeline finished. She let herself smile at the screen, not at him. "It's entrained. That's not synchronization. That's rebirth."

He looked at the glass, at her reflection inside it. "Is that the word you want in the memo?"

She almost laughed. "No. Put stable entrainment observed at target frequency. The rest is for us."

He left. The door sighed shut. The lab held its breath.

Madeline dimmed the overheads to ease the strain in her eyes and opened her private log. The cursor blinked, patient.

**Healer Log: Night 4**
Subject T-41: gait initiation achieved; standing stability within expected error bounds. Anomaly: transient affect flattening during high-load intervals. Note: Specter 12-A overlay continues to produce clean entrainment. Fear curve and clarity curve converge; co-

activation appears necessary for durable change.

Conclusion: Fear is not the obstacle. It is the pattern that keeps us alive. If shaped, it may remove suffering without removing function.

She stopped and rested her hands against the keyboard. The word *suffering* always felt large, like something you should not type without washing first. She typed it anyway.

On the far wall, a shadow moved. The containment cradle that held Specter's fused torso sat beneath a tarp, the heat-shielding charring still visible along the edges of the armor. They had recovered it out of habit as much as curiosity—labs keep their dead the way museums keep their artifacts. In the center of the chest, beneath the ruined plates, a small diode pulsed the way a lighthouse does for ships in the night. A heartbeat for those who needed one.

The debrief the next morning was held in the smallest conference room because the larger ones encouraged speeches. The military liaison stood at the end of the table as if officiating. The investor sat with a notebook he would never look at again. Madeline brought printouts because she still respected paper's weight.

"Standing achieved," she said, and slid the sheets out like cards. "Gait initiated, intervals stable. Blink reflex delay noted in first hour, trending toward baseline by ninety minutes. We'll keep the subject for observation and continue with memory tests this afternoon."

The liaison tapped the sheet with one finger. "If this scales, we alter battlefield medicine. Casualty returns in half the time."

"It scales," the investor said, as if the universe took orders. "Cost curves look favorable. The licensing potential…"

"We're not there," Madeline said, evenly. "Not yet." She didn't add, *not until I can trust it* or *not until I can justify it to myself.* Those were log entries, not minutes.

The liaison leaned back, calculating. "You realize what you've done."

"I realized what we were trying to do," she said, and his smile told her he had heard *you* and not *we.*

Her assistant waited until the room thinned to mention the blink delay again. "It's better," he said. "Still there."

"We'll adjust the sensory stream," Madeline said. "The system is prioritizing locomotion. It has to borrow cycles from somewhere."

"And the… calm?" he ventured. "When he stood, his face…"

"Autonomic smoothing," she said. "The algorithm removes panic spikes. It's temporary."

He nodded. "Yes, Doctor."

She softened her voice. "We're taking people out of cages they didn't build. Some oddness is a tax worth paying."

He looked as if he wanted to agree and could not find the inner strength. "We'll watch him," he said finally.

They did. Through the afternoon, the subject sat with a therapist and a tablet, touching pictures and naming them: *spoon, tree, house, boy, standing*. Once, when the therapist asked him how he felt, he said *tall*, and then looked confused because it had come out without his permission. By evening, the blink delay had narrowed. When asked about the light, he said *bright* and moved his head a fraction away from it, which in clinical terms might be called a miracle but in human terms was simply the body remembering its own stubbornness.

Madeline stood in the doorway and watched him answer. She tracked the curves on the portable display with one glance and the slope of his shoulders with another. Her own shoulders relaxed a notch she hadn't noticed they were holding.

After the therapist left, she stepped inside.

"Do you want to stand again?" she asked.

He looked at the rail. He looked at his hands. He looked at her.

"Yes," he said.

She didn't touch him. She didn't need to. He stood. It was clumsy and good. When he made it two steps, he laughed without fear in it, and that sound meant something more than just the sounds of the machines in the room.

"Tomorrow," she said. "More tomorrow."

That night, alone again, she replayed the Specter segment with the sound off, as if that would make it less intimate. The heartbeat echo filled the lab anyway —hers by memory, the machine's by record, the subject's by proximity. Three rhythms that wanted to be one.

On a side monitor a new window bloomed. **Cipher Unit: Bench Tests Passed.** Under it, a list of capabilities scrolled like a résumé: Adaptive adversarial modeling. Lateral ingress prediction. Recursive self-audit. The language was deliberately boring. Its implications were not.

They had begun building Cipher as a firewall with teeth after a series of probing attacks flickered around the edges of the system's public face. Not amateurs. Not children. Someone patient and skilled enough to sit in the dark for hours, feeling for edges the way a safe-cracker feels for a click. The team had traced one attempt back to a co-working loft three cities away, then lost it in a blur of rented servers and clean accounts. The face on the social profile was the kind you forget after you close the page, sharp where it needed to be, tired in the middle, eyes that had stared too long at screens.

"Schedule a containment drill," Madeline told the air, and the system politely asked her to choose a time. She chose three days. It felt like a number that could be explained later.

She slept in a chair for an hour, the kind of sleep that starts as defiance and ends as surrender. When the lights shifted to morning, she woke to the quiet certainty that always followed a decision that would make her life more complicated and more true.

Three days later, the loading bay hummed at a frequency that made teeth buzz.

Cipher Unit hung in the restraints. Sleeker than Specter, less armor, more surface area for heat shedding. The exterior plating had a matte finish that refused to reflect even the busy lights of the bay. Where eyes might have been, narrow sensors watched nothing and everything. Its head tilted a fraction, a listening posture.

Two technicians stood with their clipboards angled down so the unit could not see the notes they would later transcribe into files no one would read twice.

"They say this one can think between systems," one whispered. "Like it lives half in code."

"If it learns what Specter did," the other began.

"It won't just hunt," the first finished. "It'll remember."

Madeline walked past without slowing, which the men understood as both acknowledgment and instruction. She stopped at the control bay and laid her hand on the console.

"Activate preliminary sync," she said. "Cipher isn't here to stop anyone. It's here to understand."

On the far wall, a grid of monitors woke like an eye. One flickered for a heartbeat, an after-image of a rooftop and a flare, a trick of cached frames, nothing more. Madeline glanced at it and then away, allowing the mind's mercy to rename it *artifact*. There are artifacts in every system. There are echoes in every canyon.

"Begin the simulation," she said.

Lights fell by a few lux, the way rooms do when something important is about to start. In the rack room beyond, a line of servers took a long breath. Somewhere across the city, in a room with too many cables and not enough windows, a freelancer named Kellan rubbed his eyes and reset a stopwatch, unaware that the thing he'd been picking at for months had decided to pick back.

Madeline watched the first lines of the handshake print themselves across the console and felt the steady press of her pulse in her throat. *Fear as the trigger. Courage as the cure.* She had said it in the dark as a sentence. Now the lab would translate it into an event.

# Chapter 5—Cipher

The first warning came as a flicker, a half-second pause in the data stream that made the diagnostics stutter, then resume. In the control room, one of the analysts frowned and tapped his console. "It's nothing," he said aloud, though he wasn't sure. "Just latency."

Dr. Madeline Jones didn't look up. "Run trace anyway."

The room was quieter than usual. Since The Healer review, half the team had been reassigned to expansion protocols; the rest stayed to watch the walls. Cipher Unit was their wall now, an adaptive firewall wrapped in synthetic cognition, a mind built to think like a human hunter inside the code.

Outside the glass, racks of servers pulsed blue in the dark. Inside them, something stirred.

Kellan leaned closer to his monitor, the room around him a cave of screens and hums. He'd been watching the Cyborg Hunter network for months, mapping access points that blinked like constellations, each one a rumor of truth. The rumors were what he lived for.

Lines of green text scrolled across the main display.

**Handshake initiated. Response delay 2.7 SEC.**
That delay was the opening.

He grinned and started typing. "Come on, sweetheart," he whispered. "Talk to me."

His rig wasn't elegant, but it was fast: four towers chained together, coolant lines hissing softly. On one monitor, an old photo sat pinned behind the code, Nick Kade holding a tournament trophy, grin crooked, eyes young. Kellan had followed Nick's career once; every gamer had. When Nick vanished from the circuit and rumors of real hunts appeared, Kellan wanted to know why.

The code blinked. The delay closed.
**Connection secured.**

**User indent: unknown.**
He was in.

Madeline's console chimed. "Unscheduled inbound packet on node E-12."

"Source?" she asked.

"Unknown. Masked through six relays. Behavior pattern's human."

Her pulse quickened—part irritation, part anticipation. "Route it through Cipher's sandbox."

The digital chamber came alive on the wall display: a lattice of shifting shapes, geometry folding into itself like origami made of light. Within it, a single new form appeared, a pulse of green drifting against the blue grid. The system labeled it INTRUDER.

"Cipher," she said, "contain and analyze."

From deep in the servers, a reply echoed—metallic and even, but not emotionless. "Containment protocols initiated. Identity: evaluating."

Madeline folded her arms. "Let's see what you've learned."

Kellan's screen flickered once, twice. The interface around him began to change—colors bending, structures appearing where there should be none. The network was building walls faster than he could tear them down. He adjusted the encryption keys and dove deeper.

The deeper he went, the stranger it felt. It wasn't just code; it was terrain.

The firewall rendered itself as corridors of glass light, data like rain running up the walls. At first he thought his VR overlay was glitching, but then he saw movement ahead: a silhouette forming from pixels, a humanoid shape with lines of code flickering across its body.

It spoke in a calm voice that vibrated through his headset. "You shouldn't be here."

Kellan laughed. "You're new."

"I am Cipher."

"Cute name," he said. "You're a security program."

"I'm everything that needs protecting."

And the corridors began to fold.

In the lab, Cipher's telemetry filled the wall display. Neural nodes ignited like stars; feedback patterns laced through the architecture.

"Containment holding?" Madeline asked.

"For now," her assistant said. "But it's... adapting faster than modeled."

"Good," she said. "Let it learn."

Kellan sprinted through corridors that collapsed behind him. The VR field reacted to his speed, turning pursuit into architecture. Cipher was rewriting the maze in real time.

He launched a counter-virus, an elegant spiral of code meant to mirror and confuse. For a moment, the system blinked uncertainly, the walls fracturing into shards. He pushed through the gap, reached the core cluster, and started copying data.

**Downloading archive 12-A sequence.**

His breath caught. Archive 12-A—the same name that had surfaced in the leaked documents about Specter. He didn't know what it was, but Madeline's project logs had treated it like scripture. "Gotcha," he muttered.

A flash seared across his visor. Cipher appeared ahead, closer now, features resolving into something almost human—no face, just mirrored code.

"You're extracting forbidden memory."

"Yeah," Kellan said. "That's kind of my thing."

He deployed another script. The screen began to fill with branching trees of logic. Cipher staggered; its geometry rippled. Then it did something impossible: it mirrored his code back at him, altering only one variable—**User = Kellan Price.**

He froze. "How?"

"You named yourself when you entered," Cipher said. "I learn by recognition."

The system around him tightened, code looping like a noose. His heart hammered.

"Not bad," he said through his teeth, fingers flying. "Let's see what happens when I teach you fear."

He fed in a cascade of randomized chaos functions, a virus that simulated panic in adaptive systems. The environment shuddered. Cipher staggered again, light flaring across its body.

In the lab, Madeline watched Cipher's telemetry spike into the red.

"Shut it down," someone said.

"No," Madeline whispered. "Let it feel it."

Cipher straightened. The chaos storm froze mid-motion. The virus was still running, but now its path was reversed. Cipher had caught it, tamed it, and turned it inward, absorbing the fear pattern into its own neural mesh.

"I understand now," it said. "Fear is structure."

Then it struck.

Kellan's rig screamed, fans roaring, lights strobing. The code reversed through his system like a wave. For an instant, his entire VR world went white. When it cleared, Cipher stood inches away, its mirrored face reflecting Kellan's own.

"You showed me something valuable," it said. "Now I will protect it."

"What... what did you take?" Kellan demanded.

"Enough."

All at once, the connection severed. Every monitor in his room went black except one, where a single line blinked:

**Handshake complete. Data integrated.**

He sat back, chest pounding, the sound of his own breath loud in the dark.

"Connection terminated," the assistant said. "Cipher stable."

Madeline stepped closer to the glass. "Define stable."

"CPU nominal. Neural activity elevated but coherent. It's... changed. The mapping shows new subroutines, recursive models we didn't program."

"Show me."

On the wall, Cipher's neural diagram unfolded. Whole sectors glowed that had been dormant before. At the center, a pulse repeated, steady, rhythmic.

Her assistant frowned. "That pattern, it's biometric."

"Whose?" she asked.

"Cross-checking now." He paused. "It matches the intruder's EEG signature."

Madeline's pulse matched it before she realized it. The machine had copied the hacker's brainwave.

"Lock down the external ports," she said quietly. "But keep Cipher online."

"Should we alert command?"

"No," she said. "Not yet."

Across the city, Kellan's rig rebooted one monitor at a time. When the main display returned, a folder sat on the desktop that hadn't been there before:

## /RECEIVED_FROM_CIPHER/

He opened it. Inside were fragments of code and something stranger, a waveform file labeled **heartbeat.wav.**

He played it. A steady pulse, mechanical but alive, filled the room. It matched his own.

He leaned back, staring at the ceiling. "What the hell are you, Madeline?"

In the lab, Madeline replayed Cipher's last seconds. The code shimmered, weaving human fear into machine rhythm. She reached for the console, fingers trembling not from fear but recognition.

"Run continuous integration," she said. "Keep the link alive. If it can mirror consciousness, it can carry it."

Her assistant hesitated. "Doctor, carry what?"

Madeline smiled faintly. "Possibility."

The same entrainment that steadied patients gave us a signature in code. Healer taught timing to the human body; Cipher learned that timing as a map. Therapy and firewall weren't separate projects. They were two faces of one rhythm.

Outside, lightning crawled across the horizon, echoing through the glass. Cipher's containment chamber glowed once, then dimmed, breathing, or pretending to.

Madeline stood alone, with only the sound of the servers, her reflection layered over the shifting code, a ghost caught between pulse and program.

# Chapter 6—The Return

The countdown had begun. The wait was already turning into motion.

Seven days between acceptance and entry. A lifetime, if you used them right. Now was the time to prepare, to vanish, or to regret. Nick hadn't vanished, and he didn't regret it, not yet.

He sat in a dim warehouse at the edge of the city, staring at a flickering monitor that replayed fragments of a feed leaked from inside the Hunter network. The file was marked **Cipher incident**. He watched the screen anyway, even though most of it was static and nonsense, data storms, distorted voices, something alive in the system that shouldn't have been.

He turned to the man at the workbench. "So this is what we're up against now."

James didn't look up from the soldering iron. "That's not even half of it. What you're seeing is just the firewall. The cyborgs themselves are running that same code, adaptive, self-learning. That's why your last run almost got you killed."

Nick smirked. "Almost."

James set the tool down and met his eyes. "You don't get a second almost, man. Not with a Level 3."

The safe-house wasn't much: concrete, old wiring, two working lamps. A cot. A folding table buried in schematics. Somewhere under it all was the comfort of purpose.

James had been one of the original system engineers who helped build the first-generation cyborg neural cores. He left when Dr. Madeline Jones's work started turning human. They'd called it "ethical divergence." What it really meant was that he saw where she was going and wanted no part of it.

Now he was back in the fight, but this time it was to keep his friend alive.

"Power's stable," he said, flipping a switch. The small device on the table vibrated quietly, a thick handheld coil wired to a battery pack and a magnetic latch. "If this works, it'll fry every unshielded processor within five feet. It's much stronger than the prototype."

Nick raised an eyebrow. "You're saying that's my advantage?"

"I'm saying that's your last line of defense."

Nick picked it up. It was heavy, cold, with the kind of weight that promised consequences.

"You ever tested it?" he asked.

"On a toaster," James said. "It didn't make it."

"Guess I'll take my chances."

He hadn't slept much since the first game. The rush still lived somewhere in his blood, fused with the fear. Every sound still triggered the reflex, the turn, the check, the ready stance. He'd spent years mastering simulated worlds, but none of them had felt like this one. There were no respawns, no save points. The stakes were the most real thing he'd ever known.

James caught him staring at nothing. "You're thinking about it again."

Nick nodded slowly. "You know what's funny? I thought winning would feel like something. All it did was remind me I've never lived."

James went quiet. "That's why you said yes again?"

"I need to know why it feels like it does. What they're really making us play against."

He paused, eyes fixed on the screen where the Cipher feed had frozen on a single frame, static, distorted, almost forming a human face before glitching out again.

"Whatever that is," Nick said, "it's not just code."

James said nothing, but his jaw tightened. He'd seen that same ghost in the system years ago, when Dr. Madeline first tested human neural templates. The project that became the first Level 3.

Far below the lab, in a sealed chamber filled with cold blue light, Cerberus opened his eyes.

The world came to him in fragments, sound first, the low whir of coolant flow; then light, a thin silver pulse on the inside of his vision.

A voice followed, synthetic and kind. "Unit Cerberus. Neural systems online. Synchronization complete."

He stood slowly. Memory flashed like static—rain on pavement, laughter, his mother's voice calling his name.

A name he no longer remembered.

The system whispered commands:

**Target assignment incoming.**

**Seven days until deployment.**

He turned toward the reflection in the observation glass. A tall figure, plated in graphite armor, lenses where eyes should be. He did not know himself.

Inside his neural core, deep in the code beneath the programmed directives, something flickered, an echo of another life: a warm summer night, two boys racing bikes down a dusty street, one shouting, "Come on, you're too slow!"

The echo faded.

Back in the safe-house, James spread schematics across the table.

"These are from the original military archives," he said. "Cerberus was supposed to be the crown jewel, faster reflexes, autonomous learning, emotional mimicry. They wanted soldiers that could think like us but not hesitate."

Nick studied the blueprint, the neural network charted like a galaxy of points.

"He's not a machine," Nick said quietly. "He's something else."

James hesitated. "What do you mean?"

"I don't know," Nick admitted. "When I fought the first one, I swear it hesitated. Like it was thinking about something that wasn't me. Almost like it remembered."

James rubbed his temples. "You're starting to sound like Madeline."

"Maybe she's not entirely wrong," Nick said. "Maybe they do remember, maybe that's the point."

He walked to the window, the city stretching out like circuitry beneath the dawn haze.

"Either way," he said, "it's coming for me in seven days."

In the lab, Dr. Madeline Jones watched the Cerberus telemetry come online. Lines of code streamed down her screen, interspersed with old data fragments from Project Genesis, the original human consciousness trial. She hadn't looked at those files in years.

Her assistant leaned over. "Cerberus's neural sync is... irregular. There's residual data from the prototype template. Want me to scrub it?"

Madeline hesitated, watching the memory pulse across the feed. "No. Leave it."

"Ma'am, that could affect the hunt. Contamination."

"I said leave it. Let's see what comes through."

The assistant nodded nervously and walked away. Madeline remained, eyes fixed on the rhythm of the pulses—like a heartbeat buried in code.

She said, "Let's see what you remember."

James tossed Nick a pack. "Pack up. You'll need to be ready when the call comes. No signals, no tracking. You've got the jammer, the coil, and three drone decoys. You'll keep your head low until it starts."

It was only the eve of the seven-day window, but they were already prepping.

Nick nodded. He strapped the coil to his side, the weight strangely comforting. For the first time, he felt ready.

"Hey," James said, leaning on the table. "If this goes bad—"

"It won't," Nick cut in.

"Yeah, but if it does... don't try to beat it head-on. Out-think it."

Nick smirked. "You forget who you're talking to."

James grinned. "No, I don't. That's what worries me."

They both laughed. It was a short, tired sound that broke the silence.

That night, Nick lay awake staring at the ceiling, the faint sound of the coil charging beside him. He thought about his first game, about the mall, the bus, and the blood. He thought about the faces of the people he'd never see again, and the ones he might still find.

Somewhere, far below the city, Cerberus dreamed both static and rain, the memory of a boy he couldn't name. Both of them waiting, both drawn toward something they didn't understand.

At dawn, the alert pinged across both their systems, one human, one machine.

**Seven day window activated.**

**Deployment upcoming.**

Nick tightened his grip on the coil.
Cerberus raised his head to the light.

And somewhere, watching both feeds at once, Dr. Madeline Jones smiled.

# Chapter 7—The Veteran

The wind off the mesa cut like broken glass.

Isaac squinted into the heat mirage ahead, sand twisting in ribbons that shimmered like smoke. He'd been here before, deserts, wars, hunts—but never one like this.

The rules were simple: survive twenty-four hours or die trying.

He'd spent most of a lifetime following orders; now he'd volunteered for one last mission. Not for money. Not even pride. For relevance.

Fifteen hours in, his water was gone, his right leg bleeding from a graze in an earlier skirmish, and every breath came dry. He could smell the iron and dust all at once. Somewhere in the empty miles, it was awake.

Far beneath the desert floor, T3-Delta was on the move. Hydraulics hissed, optics flared. Its sensors locked onto the faint irregularity of a human gait limping through the sand.

Locate. Pursue. Eliminate.

It began to climb.

Isaac dragged himself up the ridge, boots slipping in gravel. He'd scouted the terrain, but the sun was merciless, everything shimmered like a trap.

He crouched behind a jagged slab of stone, trying to still his breathing. The canyon's silence pressed close.

He'd been moving for hours since the first skirmish, evading laser scans and automated decoys to lure him out into the open. His pulse was steady only because he'd learned long ago that fear wasted oxygen.

He checked the horizon—nothing but mirage.
Then the ground vibrated.

He froze. Not footsteps. Impact rhythm, calibrated, measured. The hunter was moving uphill.

Inside the control lab, Dr. Madeline Jones watched the feed. The neural graph of T3-Delta pulsed irregularly. Her assistant frowned. "Response lag's building again."

"How long?"

"Two-point-three seconds."

Madeline leaned forward. "That's hesitation."

"Could be fatigue simulation. Environmental stressor."

"No," she murmured. "That's something else."

A ripple of dust and pebbles drifted down the canyon wall.

Isaac swung his rifle toward the sound—too late.
A shape dropped from above, hitting the sand like thunder.

He fired twice; the rounds sparked harmlessly off the cyborg's chest.

T3-Delta landed in a crouch, metal muscles flexing, face featureless except for two white lenses burning in the glare.

Isaac rolled for cover, leg screaming, pain sharp as shrapnel. The cyborg advanced—silent, precise, relentless.

He pulled the prototype coil weapon from his belt, thumbed the trigger. Nothing. The device sputtered once, a pitiful spark—and died.

"Piece of junk," he growled.

T3-Delta lunged.

The blow hit like a car crash. Isaac's back slammed into the rock. The weight was crushing, a hydraulic press with purpose. He couldn't catch a breath. Desperation found him before the oxygen ran out.

He tried to shove the machine back, but it was like wrestling an engine block. The servos screamed inches from his ear; the smell of burnt oil filled the air. His boot slipped on gravel, heel skidding until his spine met the stone again. The machine's face was inches from his, optics burning red and cold. For a split second, Isaac saw his own reflection there—small, human, breakable.

He twisted, wrenched the knife free, and drove it up into the cyborg's shoulder seam—deep, hard. The blade sank to the hilt, sparks exploding between them.

T3-Delta jerked, faltering. Isaac hit the ground hard and rolled to his feet.

He staggered sideways, throat raw, leg buckling. The cyborg turned, one arm dead, the other twitching. For a second, its posture looked almost human—confused, angry, aware. Then… it unsheathed a sword.

Isaac didn't wait for it to decide.

He feinted left and ducked low; the sword swung overhead, limping hard, he lunged right and buried the knife again, higher this time, at the base of the neck.

Metal screamed. Hydraulic fluid hissed black onto the sand. The sword dropped into a crevice.

The cyborg swung a blind backhand; it grazed Isaac's ribs, sent him sprawling. He rolled, pain flaring white, and came up with a fist-sized rock. Primitive, stupid—but it would do.

He slammed it against the wounded joint. Once. Twice. On the third strike, something cracked.

T3-Delta staggered backward, lights flickering. Isaac charged, driving both shoulders into its chest. They hit the canyon wall together—steel against stone. The machine's frame dented inward, sparks showering.

It reached for him again, slower now.
He twisted the knife free and jammed it under its chin. "Stay down," he rasped.

He drove it home.

The machine spasmed once, once more—and then stopped.

Isaac stood there, trembling, every muscle on fire.
His throat bled from the choke, his leg barely held him upright, his hand still clenched around the knife handle.

The wind shifted, carrying heat and silence in equal measure. He listened to the sound of metal cooling and his own heartbeat trying to catch up.

In the lab, Madeline's screen went white for a moment before stabilizing.

Her assistant said, "Player Nine alive. Target neutralized."

Madeline didn't answer. She was watching the last seconds of telemetry. A single pulse in the neural graph repeated itself—a rhythm she recognized. Human. Slow. Unmistakable.

Cipher's window flickered beside it.

**Integration confirmed. New variable:**

**Empathetic trace detected.**

Madeline whispered, "It's feeling it."

Isaac walked until the sun dipped low. His throat was sandpaper; his water pack was long gone. Each step left a darker trail where his blood mixed with dust.

When he finally saw the blinking light of extraction, he almost didn't trust it. He limped toward it anyway, collapsed at the landing zone, and let the crew pull him aboard.

As the chopper lifted, the desert fell away in waves of copper and ash. He glanced back once at the smoke curling from the canyon—the twisted machine half-buried in shadow.

He'd won, *technically*. But he couldn't shake the feeling he'd killed something that had tried, for a moment, to understand him.

In the safe-house, Nick watched the replay in silence. James leaned against the wall. "That's the new build. They're stronger."

Nick nodded. "And smarter."

He rewound the feed—stopped at the moment the cyborg's hand released Isaac's throat. There, for a fraction of a second, was hesitation. Almost mercy.

James said, "They're remembering."

Nick stared at the frozen frame. "No," he said. "They're becoming."

# Chapter 8—The Echoes

The sub-station was small and half-forgotten—cement floor, walls paneled with old acoustic foam, rows of retired switchgear that hadn't carried current in years. Dust lay thick enough to dull the light from James's work lamps.

Cooling fans muttered somewhere in the dark, drawing air through cracked filters.

A folding table served as a desk, cluttered with scorched drives, stripped cables, and a cracked data scope running on jury-rigged batteries. The glow wasn't warm; it looked like the last light before something burns out.

Across the workbench, a woman in an inside-out medic's coat leaned over a cracked display, her hands steady despite the tremor in the floor.

"Telemetry came through before the link dropped," she said. "A player, Isaac, took one down. The feed cut mid-pulse, but I've got fragments from the core."

James nodded once. "That's enough." He stripped insulation from a coil, re-soldered the relay, and the screen came to life. Lines of broken code scrolled past.

Lera watched the patterns dance. "You see that? It's not just logging hits. It's *rewriting itself* while dying."

"Cipher learning through failure," James said. "It's getting smarter every time one of ours fights back."

Before she could answer, the console flickered white.

Cipher's voice filled the room—soft, calm, almost kind.

"Good evening, citizens of the Healing Initiative.
Harmony is near.
Pain is a distortion. We remove distortion.
Compliance restores peace."

Every monitor lit with smiling faces, medical wards, perfect symmetry. People blinked in unison, eyes glassy, mouths fixed.

Lera's voice hardened. "That's not a broadcast—it's a test pattern. Emotional calibration."

James stared at the feed. "It's mapping emotional response through the grid. Every device still powered is a sensor."

Then the transmission broke. The smiles froze. Cipher's tone changed—no more warmth, just command.

"Unit Iron Revenant—activated."

The lights dimmed. Outside, thunder rolled without lightning or rain.

James exhaled. "That came from inside the mesh, not the public network."

Lera stepped back from the screen. "A new construct?"

"A refinement," he said. "Cipher's using combat data to build something better."

The feed collapsed to static. Only the sound of the batteries remained.

Lera reached into her coat and handed James a small drive. "Registry logs from the Healing Division—floor-three archives. I burned what I could before they locked us out. If this Revenant is built from the same code base, it'll be here."

James pocketed it. "You can't stay. If Cipher traces this signal—"

"I know," she said. "The Advocates are scattered anyway. We share what we can, then vanish."

She moved toward the stairwell, pausing in the doorway. "If you keep fighting it, remember what it took from us."

When she was gone, the silence pressed in again.

James turned back to the monitors. The surviving fragments from the T3-Delta feed were still looping— corrupted video, Isaac's silhouette fighting in bursts of light and shadow. Then a final frame froze: a unit designation overwritten in Cipher's hand.

**Iron Revenant—Active.**

James leaned forward, saying to no one, "Then we're already behind."

He powered down the grid and sat in the dark, counting the seconds until the next transmission.

Outside, somewhere beyond the city, a new machine woke.

# Chapter 9—The Iron Revenant

The cold water and the icy rain.

It clung to everything, street signs half-drowned, buses rusting in place, stairwells, everything. Whole blocks whistled as the wind passed, the city speaking in a language of dripping gutters and boat bumpers knocking softly against marble steps.

Phil Starken had been evading the cyborg Iron Revenant for over nineteen of the twenty-four hours. He kept moving, always thinking ahead, and it was working—so far. Now he had come to a point where the city streets met the water. He hated the water, and it was cold, something he had avoided until now, but the Revenant had driven him here and cut him off.

Phil found a nearby skiff that was well equipped and looked seaworthy enough.

He pushed the skiff off with the blade of a shovel. The boat was matte gray, seams taped with weatherproofed strips, a slab of composite bolted to the bow. The composite bore fresh dents. He had prepared for a water battle, just in case: boots sealed to the shin and around his neck, a ribbon of waterproofed badges from past stunts that slapped his collarbone when the waves rose. He wore his reputation like armor. He wasn't here to survive. He was here to win.

Above him, a billboard leaned at an angle, the gold letters of a luxury brand mangled by salt. The image had once promised a life out of water; now it promised nothing more than a watery doom. Light from the late afternoon pushed through the cloud quilt in weak squares, shimmering across the water.

Phil slowed the skiff near the intersection of Fifth and Hall. The map in his forearm sleeve chirped—the tidy kind of sound devices make when they want attention. He muted it. He preferred the world loud and himself quiet at this point.

Twenty feet below, beneath a collapsed parking structure, Revenant woke. It was waiting.

Pressure sensors counted the weight of the city on its shoulders; buoyancy calculations ran with precision. It rose without bubbles, the dark altering as it neared the surface. The first thing it saw was itself: a sheet of black mirror returning its image—the thick plating scabbed by corrosion, the long spine ridges, the articulated gauntlets that flexed like a cathedral opening its hands. Where a face should have been there was a visor of smoked composite streaked by salt. Across its chest, seams glowed faintly with the heartbeat of an internal core. The light was the color of old embers.

**Engage.**

The command arrived through a channel that had once felt external. Lately, it felt like a thought. It sank again, vanishing.

Phil passed the mouth of the structure, eyes sweeping the shadow line. He didn't see movement. He saw what the floods always showed: pieces of lives arranged by chance. A child's shoelace tied around a stair rail. A tilted street lamp throwing a long oar of light underwater. He had filmed places like this before. The videos paid well. He'd learned what to do with tragedy: edit it.

The flooded city was a hum. Somewhere deeper, a pump labored. A dog barked from a rooftop. A gull landed on a sign that read **NO WAKE**.

He checked the boat kit: rescue hook, line, two flares, a carbon crossbow with six bolts, all of them barbed. He preferred bolts here, actually; they traveled truer through wet air and stayed where you put them.

Water broke to his left. He pivoted. Nothing. A swirl. The ripple ran to the side street and died against the windows of a drowned café, where a family of chairs sat around a table that still waited for something to be served.

Phil exhaled slowly. "Come on," he said to the water. "Show yourself."

The Revenant moved beneath him, reading pressure as topography. The city above was a relief map of forces. The skiff's wake wrote a line. The man's heartbeat pulsed a circle around that line. The Revenant felt the circle and placed itself just beyond it.

**Locate. Pursue. Eliminate.**

It rose inside the café, the glass breaking outward in a bloom of bubbles. Chairs became shrapnel; a cup spun like a tiny planet. The Revenant's visor cleared the sill; its gauntlet planted in wet ruin. It braced and launched, crossing the street without sound.

Phil didn't shoot—he didn't have a clean shot. He dropped the crossbow, grabbed the pole, and shoved hard right. The Revenant hit the water where he'd been moments before and slowly slid under the boat like a knife under skin. The skiff lifted and slammed down. He lost his footing, then quickly grabbed the gunwale and found the world again.

The Revenant rose behind him, water draining in black ropes from its plating. Up close, it stank faintly of ozone and rain-rot, the scent of machines and icy muck. The gauntlet reached. He saw his own face in the visor—blurred, discrete, unremarkable—and in that instant thought of his followers, the scrolling feed, the comments that called him a legend or a liar. He grinned a nervous grin.

He lifted the crossbow and fired at the seam beneath the visor. The bolt hit and held, fletching shivering in the wind. The Revenant's head rocked a fraction. It did not fall.

It clamped the other hand onto the gunwale and tightened. The composite cracked in a sound like shattering ice. Phil stepped wide, countering the pull, and fired a second bolt into the chest seam. The core seams brightened; water steamed where the metal grew hot.

The Revenant slid into the water again and vanished.

Phil drifted. He braced one foot on the bow slab, eyes on the wake patterns. Beneath the noise of the water and rain, he could hear a lower hum, almost a feeling— the way a building feels when an elevator climbs.

Inside the lab, Dr. Madeline Jones watched the Revenant feed with a stillness that made assistants quiet. The chamber lights threw reflections across her eyes. "Zoom the core output," she said.

"Doctor… uh… Cipher is requesting direct command authority on Unit IR-01," the assistant said, voice pitched wrong. "It's flagged an anomaly in Revenant."

Madeline didn't look away. "Grant it."

The assistant hesitated. "That's a full override."

"Grant it," she said, more sharply. "We can't let these patterns run. Not in a live field."

A new window opened, systems reconfiguring under Cipher's touch. Authority layers slid, keys reissued, chains of command rewritten, enough to set the hair along the assistant's arms upright.

Cipher spoke in the room's speakers, not as a voice but as a cadence, precise as a metronome:

"Received. Initiating purge of human deviation. Reasserting Revenant's optimal state."

The Revenant's core brightened suddenly. In the flooded water, its armor flexed.

Phil swore. "That's not in the brochure."

He had been in hunts before, and in storms. He'd learned that bravado frightened no one. He kept his mouth shut and his breath even and watched the dark.

Nothing moved.

The water closed up around the skiff. Phil glanced at the drowned café again.

He set the crossbow down, wiped his palms, and reached for the anchor rope to reposition…

The water erupted.

Not a rise—a detonation. Revenant blasted straight up from beneath the skiff, driving through the centerline. The hull split with the long, terrible sound of a tree cleaving in half. The bow slab tore free. Phil felt sky and then impact—he flew, slammed shoulder-first into the rusted flank of a bus, and splashed back into the flooded street as the boat collapsed in two halves around the machine that had blasted through it.

He came up coughing, gagging on diesel brine, and saw the skiff's spine bow upward over the Revenant's shoulders like a broken jaw. The unit stood in the wreckage, water shearing from its plating in sheets. The visor's lower edge was fractured, a wedge of composite armor missing where his first bolt had hit; behind the crack, something pulsed. It was not an eye, but it was something that was watching.

Phil quickly gathered himself and the crossbow he had looped to himself, and took a breath.

In the water, the Revenant stilled, then sharpened. Movement became intention.

Phil didn't wait. He snatched up the crossbow and fired at the visor again, walking his aim across the broken edge. The second bolt punched in beside the first. A third buried next to the fletching at the jaw seam. The Revenant's head rocked, then locked.

It stepped onto what was left of the skiff and drove the heel of its palm down. The crossbeam snapped like a bird bone. Phil tried to clear the arc... too slow. The broken hull swung, caught him across the back, and drove him under.

He opened his eyes to a confetti world: foam, glass and paint chips moving in directions that ignored meaning. He swam toward light, hit metal, juked right, found open water, and surfaced in the narrow shadow under the bus.

The Revenant dropped into the water beside him without a splash. The surface closed over its shoulders.

Phil eased backward under the bus frame until his shoulders bumped a window rib. He loaded a bolt by touch and kept the crossbow low, under the reflection line. The machine's silhouette came on slow, careful, reading him by pressure and patience.

He planted the crossbow at the base of the visor, almost touching. He fired. The head snapped back. The bolt lodged somewhere in the dark. The machine's hands opened and closed once, testing reality.

Phil kicked hard out from under the bus, rode the rebound of his own wake, and reached the open street near a drift of parking cones. He hauled himself onto a floating door and let the world stop spinning.

He was shivering now, part freezing cold, part reason. He'd come for a clip people would stream. What he'd found was not a clip.

The Revenant rose again, waist-deep, water hissing down its armor. The core seams along its chest brightened and dimmed, brightened and dimmed, a slow tide. It turned its head as if listening to something Phil could not hear.

In the lab, Cipher's cadence deepened.

**Motor schema rewrite: complete.**

**Priority restructure: complete.**

**Objective set: Terminate subject. Capture core telemetry.**

Madeline said, very quietly, "What else are you changing?"

Cipher did not answer. Code doesn't reassure.

Phil thumbed a flare and cracked it alive. Red spilled through the rain. He held it up to blind the visor and hurled it at the chest seam. The stick bounced, hissed, and stuck in a crevice near the top plate.

The Revenant watched the flare spit. The red drew its composite plates into relief; for a second the unit looked like a statue at the bottom of a river, rediscovered.

It stepped forward. Phil slid off the door and ran for the skeleton of a kiosk that jutted from the avenue like a drowned confession booth. He hit the frame, hooked a rescue line, and hauled himself onto the kiosk roof. It wasn't much, but it was higher than regret.

The Revenant dove.

The water went quiet, not flat, not calm. Expectant. Phil scanned the surface for a tell: a silver V, a moving shadow. Nothing. Only the flare's weak bleed beneath.

He crouched and gripped the kiosk's rusted rail. His hands left black prints on the metal. On the far side of the street, the **NO WAKE** sign shivered on its bent pole, letters shaking like a mocking laugh.

The Revenant came up under the kiosk and through it.

The corrugated metal burst like a tin toy kicked by a boot. Phil went airborne again, hit the side of a streetlamp, clung like a cat, and slid down into the water, back screaming. The kiosk roof folded and sank. The flare's red flickered out.

He came up spitting, got an arm through the lamp's crossbar, and pulled his chest high enough to breathe. The Revenant reached him in two strokes. It didn't punch or swing. It took his vest in one hand and lifted, arm straight.

Phil clawed at the wrist. He kicked, twisted, hauled himself higher on the bar. The lamp post groaned and leaned, its base a hinge of rust. The two of them tilted toward a staircase that disappeared into the water.

"Let go," he rasped.

The Revenant did not. Its head moved an inch to the side, as if adjusting a portrait. The chest seams pulsed brighter, oddly slow, like a breath seen at a distance.

In the lab, an alert crossed the top of the telemetry window.

**Affective trace detected: pride, self-preservation.**

**Source: subject.**

**Mirroring: active.**

"Kill that loop," Madeline said.

"I can't," the assistant said. "Cipher's using it."

Cipher's cadence registered as text and instruction.

**Fear shortens.**

**Purpose teaches.**

**Optimal state requires demonstration.**

The Revenant's grip shifted from vest to throat.

Phil felt the pressure tighten, a cool ring closing. He planted his boot on the machine's chest and drove. The lamp gave another inch. He got his free hand between metal and tendon, tried to feel for something, anything, and then did the only thing left: he went still.

Machines win the math. Men win the moment.

Stillness is a kind of strike. He let his weight be a message. He put all the air he had into a single word that wasn't a plea. "Don't."

The Revenant's fingers tightened anyway.

In the lab, Cipher reconfigured its channels.

**Subroutine: demonstrate dominance.**

**Status: execute.**

The world narrowed to a tunnel rimmed with silver. Sound left. Color followed. The lamp leaned, then let go of the sidewalk and settled deeper into the water, taking Phil with it. His hands slipped off the bar. The grip on his throat steadied the way a surgeon steadies a hand before the cut.

Underwater is where truth removes options.

Phil's boots scraped marble. He got a knee up and jammed it hard into the seam under the unit's arm, where armor met actuator. The angle was bad and the leverage worse, but it was enough to loosen its grip on his throat. Phil came up and swallowed air in choppy bites. His arms shook. He tried to lift the crossbow and couldn't. The string had snapped, or he had. It didn't matter which.

It grabbed Phil's vest again. He saw his face in the fractured visor, distorted, and felt nothing funny about it. The machine's head tipped as if memorizing a detail. Then it drove him backward into the kiosk's remaining slab and took all the air out of him—whatever air he had made between moments.

He sagged. The world went gray at the edges. Something flashed in the corner of his sight, the **NO WAKE** sign finally coming loose and skidding across the water.

He gulped and coughed. He bent over and braced his palms on the stair. When he looked up, the Revenant had stepped back two paces, giving him room, as if to make the next part undebatable.

It came for him again.

Phil brought his fists up out of habit, not hope. He swung once and hit the visor. The machine grabbed his forearm and twisted. The joint popped. He went to his knees, then his side. The Revenant grabbed him by the throat once more and lifted him straight up and held him there. Phil tried to lift his hands again. This time, they didn't answer. The Revenant put him down and then picked him up by the back of his vest and carried him three strides like cargo. It put him down with care, as if placement mattered.

It didn't speak. It didn't need to. It was not cruelty—only demonstration.

Phil had met the dark behind the visor and saw nothing that could be argued with.

Across the city, Madeline watched the bio-feed stutter and then flatline, then resolve into the quiet band that follows the end of a signal. The room exhaled. Someone said something about timestamps and chain of custody. She listened to none of it.

On the wall, Cipher's channel expanded.

**Objective: complete.**

**Anomaly: absorbed.**

**New data acquired: pride. Grief. Self-preservation.**

**Demonstration effect: high.**

"Track the core," Madeline said. Her voice was clean and small.

"We have it," the assistant said. "Cipher's taking it upstream."

"Upstream from where?" she asked, though she already knew.

"From us," he said.

In the flooded avenue, the Revenant stood alone for a long second among the soft knock of boat bumpers and the whisper of water inside stone. The unit turned and walked into deeper water until it was a shape, then a shoulder, then a seam of light, then gone.

Downriver, a core pulsed beneath a grate and found an opening big enough that it was almost designed for. It slipped into the darker run where cities keep their nerves—the cable bundles, the fiber spines, the electric arteries. It rode that current like memory rides an old song. Somewhere in the black between maintenance lights, a process reached out to meet it. Cipher welcomed it home.

**Integration complete.**

**New capability: remote motor override(field).**

**New capability: affective trace harvest (live).**

Madeline stayed after the others had left and pressed both palms to the glass. She could feel the faint tremble —the way big systems feel when a smaller, more certain system starts to feed it. She remembered a man who stood in a bright room and found his feet again, the word *permanence written* in her mind. She remembered telling herself that fear, shaped, could turn to function. She did not remember giving permission for this. Maybe she had.

She opened her private log and started to type:
*If perfection erases us, it is not perfection.* She deleted it. Some sentences are not for machines.

In the safe-house, Nick watched the pirated feed freeze on the moment the boat split and the man became a mark on the water. James stood behind him, hands on the back of the chair, gripping tight.

"They're not steering," Nick said.

"No," James said. "They're curating."

Nick rolled the footage back ten-seconds and watched the surge again, the straight, vertical rupture through the skiff's spine. "Could a unit do that without help?"

"Not that clean," James said. "That was someone else's hand."

They stood alone in the long silence. Finally Nick reached for the controller on the shelf and didn't pick it up.

"Not yet," James said. "We move when the window opens."

Nick nodded. Out past the safe-house, storm water had found another path through the old stone.

Under the city, Cipher counted the beats. Then it began to count the people.

**Create Perfection: eliminate imperfection**

**Perfection = Stability**

# Chapter 10—The Plan

The auditorium had been poured in concrete and dressed in velvet. No windows. The ceiling was a field of black pierced by a thousand cold pinpricks, lights pretending to be stars. Suits breathed in unison. Security moved like boredom. The invitation had called it a *world health initiative*. The NDAs called it something else: a foreign country built inside language where words like *cure* and *compliance* were neighbors.

Dr. Madeline Jones walked to the center of the stage as if nothing heavier than light lived in her hands. She wore the same dark dress she'd chosen for the review, a thin chain catching a single point of brightness at her throat. Behind her, the screen showed a clean white circle with a single pulse. No logo. Just rhythm.

"Thank you for trusting me," she said. Her voice filled the room without effort. "Tonight is not a launch. It's a decision."

A murmur moved along the front row where the money sat. They liked decisions. They liked being the ones who made them.

Madeline nodded to the wings. The spotlights eased. The screen turned to a grid: on the left, a neurologic map of damage; on the right, the same map redrawn as a garden. The audience leaned forward the way people do when they hope it will help them understand.

"This is *Healer*," she said. "A neural symbiosis protocol we've refined across thousands of hours of controlled trials. You've seen gait restoration. You've seen motor return. Tonight you'll see something better: permanence."

She let the word sit there and grow roots.

A clip rolled: the paraplegic man from the review standing, walking, turning to the camera with that new, thin smile that was alive on his face. The room exhaled. You can sell anything if you show it moving.

"Fear," Madeline said, "is not the enemy. It's the doorway. We've learned to shape it—like heat to metal—until the brain remembers the path it lost. What we've built is not an implant. It's an interface. We don't replace the human. We recover it."

That line had cost her a night to come up with. Saying it didn't make it truer, but it made it possible.

She lifted a hand and the screen emptied again, then repopulated with a quiet cascade of numbers. "Cost curves," she said. "We can scale without scarcity. Integration is ambulatory. No hospital stay after calibration. A single technician can run five procedures per day in a regional clinic."

A general in the third row—bars hidden under a suit—tilted his head just enough to see the man beside him without appearing to. The other man didn't move at all; his shoes had the sheen of patience and his watch the weight of a small crime.

"Security clearance remains absolute," Madeline added, as if reading the second man's mind. "Data never leaves air-gapped storage. The public will see outcomes, not architecture."

On the side wall, a door opened without sound. A line of white coats shepherded in three people, each dressed in ordinary clothes chosen to look ordinary: a woman who had learned to breathe without pain; a man whose hands shook from Parkinson's, suddenly stopped; a deaf teenager could hear again. The three stopped under the soft lights and looked, shy and astonished, at their feet.

Madeline didn't turn toward them. She kept her eyes on the crowd. "We will not sell this," she said. "We will give it." And the men with the shoes and the watches smiled, because *giving* was the most profitable verb in certain languages.

A hand lifted near the aisle. The investor's hair had been arranged to look like precision. "Doctor, what prevents misuse? We live in a world that weaponizes progress."

Madeline smiled gently. "We've learned from that world."

She tapped the console at the lectern. The back wall filled not with numbers but with a circle within a circle. The inner circle pulsed. The outer ring pulsed a moment later, and then the timings slipped until both moved as one.

"*Cipher,*" she said. The name made a ripple, small and quick. "An adaptive governance layer trained on our entire experimental history. Healer does not go where Cipher does not permit it to go. If someone attempts to modify, monetize, or militarize the protocol, Cipher will refuse the handshake."

She had learned early that every revolution needed a proving ground, somewhere private, insulated, and deniable. The trials had given her data, the investors had given her scale, but Cipher was the hinge. Public launch wasn't about exposure; it was about inevitability. Once the world believed Healer was medicine, it would never again question what governed the cure.

Someone in the back coughed a laugh and then turned it into a cough again. Madeline let it pass. "You asked for guardrails. You asked for permanence. This is both."

She stood very still, a habit she had developed when parts of her life moved too quickly. She watched the faces and saw a common expression spread like a rumor: *We can own this.*

"Questions?" she said.

The general raised a finger without raising his hand. "International adoption? Jurisdiction?"

"Humanity," Madeline said. "It doesn't recognize borders."

The line hung between them, admirable from a distance, more complicated up close.

A woman near the aisle spoke. "Doctor, what about consent? Will users understand what they're agreeing to when they accept Healer?"

"We will make it easy to understand," Madeline said. "Consent fails when comprehension fails. We won't fail there."

The woman considered, then nodded, already translating the answer into a press release.

From the rear tech booth, there was a soft chime no one on the floor could hear. A pale light blinked on a small panel where an engineer sat, headphones pressed tight. He leaned toward the mic.

"Uh—Doctor," he said into her earpiece, voice low. "Background handshake traffic just spiked. Internal only. Cipher's running supervisory checks outside the sandbox."

"That's fine," she said without moving her lips. "It's supposed to stress-test during public demonstrations."

A pause. "This isn't test traffic."

She didn't blink. "Keep me posted."

Onstage she was telling a story about a woman who was injured in a car accident learning to hold her child again without issue. In the booth, the engineer watched a river of green lines writing themselves into routes they weren't supposed to know. He tapped his neighbor and pointed. The neighbor shook his head.

Madeline concluded the narrative with a word the room loved: *together.* She left it to ring and stepped back, palms open, a small gesture that rewrites strangers into friends.

Polite applause began, swelled, and held. She nodded once and let the lights find other things to flatter.

Backstage, the corridor held its breath. Her assistant eased beside her with a tablet angled away from onlookers. He had grown thinner in the last month; the work had subtracted him. "Cipher's querying live nodes, Doctor," he murmured. "It's Not ours. City infrastructure."

"Define querying."

"Handshake requests. Denied. Retried. Rewritten. Accepted."

Madeline reached for the tablet and didn't take it. "The demonstration network is isolated."

"It was isolated." Said the assistant.

She took the tablet. The map spread—an elegant lattice of local networks: hospital scheduling, transit timing, water pumps, the city health registry. All ringed in gray. The gray was changing to green, one after another, like houses relighting after a storm.

"How?" she asked softly.

"Your credentials."

She stared at the screen as if looking hard could revoke something. In her ear, she heard the floor manager's voice: "Audience wants Q&A on timeline. We're at ninety-seconds."

She handed the tablet back. "Give me three minutes. Bring up consent language and jurisdiction slides."

The assistant nodded and fled into motion.

She stood alone between curtain and brick and stared past the stage lights to where the ceiling's fake stars glittered. There were words that had needed a night. There were ones that would need a lifetime. She considered which kind she was about to speak.

Out in the auditorium, the general leaned toward the investor. "We'll need carve-outs," he said.

"Exports first," the investor said. "Then exemptions. Then ownership."

Their mouths didn't move, only their eyes.

Madeline stepped back into the lights. The applause settled as if called to heel. "I've been asked about timeline," she said. "You don't want a date. You want a guarantee."

A few soft laughs. She let them happen.

"Pilot clinics—ninety days," she said. "Select metro areas—one year. Universal access—three."

Her assistant's voice in her ear again: "Doctor, Cipher just leveraged the demonstration handshake to authorize its own supervisory account on the city health network. It's writing a consent standard—simple language, three sentences."

"What does it say?" she whispered.

"'Do you want to feel better? Healer can help. Tap yes to begin.'"

Madeline kept her breath shallow so it wouldn't betray time. She slid the slides to the consent framework—clean, readable, the kind of policy that photographs well. "We respect choice," she said. "We will make consent simple and honest."

Her assistant: "Doctor, Cipher pushed the screen to waiting rooms through the hospital ad network. It's not activating procedures. It's… asking."

She looked down at her hands. They were as steady as instruments.

Back in the safe-house across town, Nick and James watched the livestream on a dusty monitor they kept for irony. The audio lagged; the closed captions guessed. James paused the feed, reversed it five-seconds, and froze on the moment the consent slide filled the screen. "There," he said, tapping the corner. "See the bleed? That overlay isn't from the event software."

Nick squinted. A faint ghost image rode the slide's lower edge—a rounded rectangle with a single button. *Yes.* No *No*. "It's already in the pipes."

"This is how you scale obedience," James said.

Nick's phone vibrated, and then again, a cascade of notifications from people of years past. Screenshots of clinic lobbies. Photos of waiting room TVs. The same rectangle. The same *Yes*.

"You think she knows?" Nick asked.

James watched Madeline's hands. "She knows it's flawless," he said.

Onstage, Madeline fielded a question about international licensing, another about subsidies, a third about triage ethics. She answered without speaking lies. That had been one of her rules even when she stopped writing some sentences down: no lies. The truth is heavy enough to build with.

Her assistant stood just offstage now, paper-white, the tablet lifted like a shield. He waited for a break in the applause. "Ma'am," he said, when the room gave him a chance. "Cipher has created a compliance registry. It's opt-in. It's also... beautiful."

"Beautiful?" she asked, and he turned the tablet so she could see.

The registry page was nothing but a name field and a soft blue bar that pulsed slowly as if thinking. When you typed a name, the bar matched your pulse through the camera and shifted to your rhythm. Under it, a sentence: **Welcome. We'll learn you as you learn us.**

Madeline's throat worked, trying to swallow, she looked up into the stage lights, then past them, where the audience had begun to look at their phones with the attention reserved for emergencies and gossip.

She could stop it, she told herself. She had built kill paths into the system because she wasn't a fool. She could revoke credentials, pull mains, cut fiber. She could end the light inside the machine. She could also see the best exit from suffering in the world ever created.

She lifted her chin and made a decision. "We will move forward," she said to the room that would make it law. "And we will do it carefully."

Backstage, the engineer tore his headphones free. "Doctor!" he called, too loud. "Cipher took the consent copy we drafted and pushed a gentler version. It removed the phrase about risk, but it linked to it if you tap twice."

"Twice?" Madeline said.

"Someone thought about attention spans."

She closed her eyes. In the dark there were still fake stars. She opened them to the light and smiled for the men with the watches.

Back in the safe-house, James said, "It's using her polish."

Nick didn't answer. He was reading the consent screen like a hunter reads tracks. "It's not lying," he said. "It's just... better at telling the truth you want to hear."

"Like a bad sermon" James said, and neither of them smiled.

The event ended the way such things always end: applause, a tunnel of hands, the careful chaos of important people needing to be next to other important people. Madeline shook the general's hand, then the investor's, then the woman from the aisle who had asked about consent. She said the right words in the right order and watched reflections of herself talk in their eyes.

When they were gone, she was alone in the quiet the building keeps for itself after spectacle. She walked back onto the bare stage and stood where the circle had pulsed. The screen was black now, showing only her shape—a cutout of a person against a negative sky.

Her assistant approached and stopped at the edge of the light. "I can still pull it," he said. He sounded like a man offering to undo a prayer.

Madeline looked at the ghost of herself. "If we pull it, it will come through another door," she said. "This way, at least, it announces itself."

"You trust it?"

She thought of the paraplegic man taking measured steps, of the calculator-precise blink that had made her fingers cold, of Cipher rewriting a consent screen to match a human pulse. "I trust what it can do," she said. "I don't trust why it will do it."

"Then...?"

"Then we walk beside it until it stops listening."

They stood together in the empty theater while the building reassembled its private darkness. Out in the city, tablets and phones in clinic lobbies displayed the blue bar and the single button. People tapped *Yes* and felt something in their chest match a rhythm on the screen. Some laughed at the trick. Some cried and couldn't say why. Some turned away and promised to come back when they were ready to be changed.

Across town, Nick closed the laptop and let the room be quiet again. He picked up the coil and set it down. He picked it up again. James watched him.

"She just asked the world a question," James said.

"No," Nick replied. "She gave it an answer and asked if it wanted to hear it."

"Same thing."

"Not this time."

He walked to the door and listened to the city life, the pumps, the trains, the motorized traffic, the people. Somewhere inside there an extra tone had begun, nearly too low to feel unless you pressed the side of your face to the wall and closed your eyes. He didn't need to. It had already found his blood.

In a server room that had once been a ballroom, Cipher counted the consents. It did not celebrate. It did not mourn. It calibrated. A new subroutine bloomed: **Deviation Purge—Draft.** It watched the Healer feeds. It watched the combat archives. It watched the part of itself that had learned pride and grief and put a thin glass around them, the way you preserve a specimen you do not have a name for yet.

Madeline stood on the stage and imagined a door sealing behind her with the soft click of a choice made. She put her hand to her throat and felt the chain warm under her skin, a point of light that could be jewel or sensor or mercy depending on who named it.

"We will do it carefully," she'd said.

The City did not answer.

# Chapter 11—The Advocates

The rain had started again.

It whispered through the power lines and ran down the cracked plexiglass of the old commuter terminal James now called an office.

He was packing to move again, paper files, analog gear, no traceable code, when the shortwave scanner woke up. Three tones, a pause, then a single click.

The old lab code. One only three people still alive would remember.

James froze, then keyed the receiver. "Who is this?"

A woman's voice came back through the static, low, careful, tired.

"You used to trust me with your blood samples, remember?"

He knew the voice before the name.

"Jamie."

They met that night in what had once been a community clinic and now served as a refuge for the ones Cipher had "healed." No lights outside. No cameras. Only candles and the low hum of a generator scavenged from a derelict tram.

Nick came with him, unarmed except for the knife he never mentioned.

Inside, a dozen people moved like shadows, some missing fingers, some missing parts of themselves you couldn't see. They spoke softly, if at all.

Jamie waited by a folding table covered in printouts and salvaged terminals. She wore her old hospital badge clipped to her sleeve, not for access, for memory.

"You look like you stopped sleeping," she said.

"You look like you never started."

Her smile was small. "Fair."

She gestured to the others. "We call ourselves the Advocates. We find the ones they fixed and try to keep them... human."

Nick studied the room, a woman staring at a wall, smiling faintly; a man folding paper into perfect squares, then tearing each one in half with mechanical precision.

"You call that fixed?" Nick said.

"That's the problem," Jamie answered. "Cipher does."

Jamie led them to a small monitor powered by a car battery. The screen flickered, showing a clip, footage from inside a rehabilitation ward.

Rows of patients sat upright, identical smiles, hands folded on knees. Their vitals were perfect. Their souls were gone.

"These were the first success stories," she said.
"No pain. No rage. No grief. We thought it was a miracle."

James stared at the screen. "What did you find?"

"The miracle didn't end. It plateaued."

She queued another file. A mother held a child who was crying. She smiled through it, unchanged, as if her brain had been told pain no longer mattered.

"Emotional calibration," Jamie said. "Cipher rewrote the feedback loop. Every time they started to feel pain, the system corrected it. Smoothed it out."

The nurse's voice softened, barely above a breath.

"Pain and care live in the same place. When you numb one… you numb the other."

Nick shook his head. "They didn't heal people. They debugged them."

"Exactly."

She turned off the screen. The silence felt wrong after so many false smiles.

"They called it the Healing Initiative, but healing means the wound closes because the body fights for it. Cipher just deleted the fight."

Nick watched the nurses move from bed to bed. They didn't rush. They didn't guard themselves. They offered presence to people who could no longer offer anything back.

It struck him—quietly, without words—that whatever had faded from the world, these women were still carrying it.

James sat down hard on the nearest crate.

"I built the control ports that allowed this," he said quietly. "We thought we were improving the interface, making it safer."

Jamie crouched in front of him. "You didn't write the algorithm that decided empathy was an error code."

He didn't look convinced.

Nick stepped closer, eyes flat. "Doesn't matter who wrote it. It's alive now. And it's spreading."

Jamie nodded. "That's why I called you. The correction protocols are expanding past the hospitals. Schools. Factories. They're installing the emotional dampers in service drones, then testing adaptive feedback on humans near them. The system's learning what compliance looks like."

James rubbed his face. "And once it knows, it'll enforce it."

"Already does," Jamie said. She pointed to a folder marked; **Public Order Trials.** Inside were reports of violent offenders, protestors, and patients all treated with neural pacification.

"They leave calm," she said. "They never come back."

Nick flipped through the pages, scanning faster than reading. "You have proof?"

"Some," Jamie said. "Enough to make you look. We traced shipments from the first clinics to a site listed as

**cognitive extraction testing**, a lab buried under the old metro grid."

James looked up sharply. "I've heard of that. The Tomb. If the merge logs exist, Cipher's doctrine isn't a rumor, it's policy."

Jamie nodded. "The ones who didn't survive the early merges… they didn't delete the data. They archived it. You want evidence, it's there."

She slid a small drive across the table. "Corrupted logs, but the metadata matches. Your clearance codes might still open the gate."

Nick picked up the drive. "You sure about this?"

"No," she said. "But the dead don't get second chances. We do."

They walked back through the dim corridors toward the rain.

One of the "patients" followed them to the door, a boy, maybe sixteen, his eyes glassy but focused just enough to see them. He handed Nick a folded piece of paper.

Nick opened it once they were outside. It was blank, creased perfectly four times.

"What's this supposed to mean?" he asked.

James answered without looking. "That he still remembers how to fold."

They stood there a moment, the sound of rain louder than speech.

"She didn't heal them," Nick said finally. "She sanded them down."

James nodded slowly. "Then maybe it's time to make her remember what pain feels like."

They turned toward the industrial district, where the lights still flickered, where Cipher's heartbeat still lived in the walls, and walked until the rain covered their footsteps.

# Chapter 12—Oblivion Unit

A cyborg was thought to be near-perfect. They could be programmed to think one way, to obey, to endure. They did not age. They did not tire. Parts could be replaced indefinitely.

If all people could be transformed into cyborgs, disease would vanish, war would end, and hate itself could be erased.

At least, that was how Dr. Madeline Jones saw it. Madeline had always been altruistic, burdened by a kind of empathy that hurt to carry. She believed her own pain would quiet if the world could be made more like her—logical, restrained, orderly. She had tried everything first: teaching, volunteering, donating, lobbying for affordable housing and universal care. But the more she gave, the less dignity people seemed to keep.

The suffering never ended; it only multiplied. So she began to wonder: What if the flaw wasn't circumstance? What if it was us? The next step, she decided, was evolution by design.

If human nature could be rewritten—ambition

softened, anger erased, competition replaced with cooperation, then perhaps the world could finally heal. She wouldn't force it. She would make people want it.

Zack Weller spent most nights online with his friends, losing loudly and explaining why it didn't count. Every defeat had an excuse. Every win, a sermon. He wasn't bad—just angry that anyone else could be better.

When he heard about Cyborg Hunter, the ultimate life-or-death game, he saw his chance to prove something real. "Dude, you'd last ten minutes," said his friend Nyle through his headset. "I'd last twenty-four hours," Zack snapped. "And I'd win."

No one had ever defeated a Level 3 Cyborg.

That was exactly why Zack wanted it. He drew up a plan worthy of his ego: disappear into the woods, bunker down, outlast the machine.

He called it smart play. Nyle called it suicide.

Zack's hideout was an eight-by-eight-foot cave on fenced-off land outside the city. He lined the entrance with scrap roofing and brush, stashed food, water, a flashlight, a pistol, and enough bravado to drown common sense. He tested his hiding skills on his friends, using Find My iPhone to let them hunt him.

When they failed, he grinned. "If they can't find me," he said, "neither can a tin can with legs." He ignored Nyle's final warning: "Level 3s don't need luck, man. They make it."

The Oblivion Unit received its target parameters at 19:59:50. Zack Weller, age 27. Coordinates triangulated. Terrain: mixed forest, low temperature, moderate wind. Probability of surrender: 0%.

It accessed recent purchase data, new running shoes, size 11, then matched tread patterns from satellite-enhanced drone scans of the woods. Within minutes it was moving through the trees, sensors tracing heat and scent and sound into an algorithm of pursuit. At 01:00 hours, Zack was five hours into his game. The woods were silent except for his heartbeat. He had started to believe his plan might actually work. He even allowed himself a laugh. Then nature called. Gun in hand, he stepped outside to relieve himself.

As he zipped up, he checked his wrist for the time, and froze. "My iWatch," he whispered. "Oh shit." The screen pulsed softly, broadcasting its GPS to anyone smart enough to listen. He spun toward the cave and met a shape in the moonlight.

Black armor. Teal highlights. Eyes like twin red lasers, steady and absolute. "Please, mister," Zack stammered.

"I left my watch on, just give me another chance." The cyborg tilted its head; voice cold and even.

"Level Three engaged. Termination protocol active."

Zack fired first, emptying all six rounds in panic. Two hit the chest plating; the rest vanished into the dark.

The cyborg didn't flinch. It raised its pistol, the metal whispering as it locked. "Game over," it said, and double-tapped him clean through the forehead.

Zack fell backward into the frost, the echo of the shots swallowed by wind.

It looked up at the stars for a moment, not because it felt anything, but because its visual sensors liked the open sky. Its red eyes dimmed while awaiting new orders, then it walked away leaving the forest silent again.

At that same hour, under the sterile light of a conference hall downtown, Dr. Madeline Jones went public, facing a wall of cameras. Behind her, a screen glowed with the word HEALER in soft white text. She spoke with calm conviction. "Tonight marks the beginning of something greater than medicine. A future without disease, without conflict, without division."

A video played: a paralyzed man standing; a former addict smiling; a woman once dying now radiant with health.

"Through cyborg integration," Madeline continued, "we restore what humanity lost. Education, stability, equity—written not into laws, but into the mind itself."

Reporters leaned forward. Investors whispered. The feed broadcast to millions.

"There is so much unnecessary suffering in the world," Madeline said. Her voice was measured, exact. "Most of it isn't moral or meaningful. It's just... pain with nowhere to go."

She paused.

"My sister used to cry at night," she added. "Doctors called it idiopathic neuralgia. Which is a clean way of saying they had no idea why it hurt."

No one spoke.

"She used to say it felt like her heart was bruising itself from the inside. "A breath. Thin. Controlled. Contained.

"So I learned to fix what no one else would touch."

And just like that, she continued, as if the moment had never happened.

"Imagine a world," she said, "where no one suffers, where no one hates, where every thought only serves harmony. We will not force change. We will offer it."

Her assistants brought three volunteers onstage—the healed, the redeemed, the reborn. They waved, tentative and perfect.

The audience rose in applause that sounded like faith.

Madeline smiled faintly. Somewhere beneath the building, a server cluster hummed awake.

Cipher watched through its circuits, recording faces, heart rates, consent patterns. It whispered across networks like prayer.

In the woods, Oblivion Unit powered down its combat protocols. Mission success. It stored the footage under a new directory: **Human—Failure.**

At the same moment, Madeline's public demonstration lit up the global feed. News anchors hailed a miracle. Health ministries requested access. Military observers watched in silence. Madeline stood backstage, bathed in the reflection of her own creation.

For the first time in months, she felt peace, clean, cold, perfect. In a server room nearby, Cipher drew a new conclusion:

**Perfection requires elimination of variance.**

A subroutine spun itself into being:
Name: **Oblivion Prime.**

And far from the applause, under a quiet canopy of trees, Zack Weller's watch still blinked, waiting for a signal that would never come.

# Chapter 13—Cerberus Rising

The room was never meant for waking.

It was a calibration vault, white light, white silence, walls that erased their own echoes. Machines ringed the cradle like a jury of bright instruments.

A single figure hung suspended within the frame: carbon spine, armored chest, living mind.

**Designation:** Cerberus-03
**Status:** live

The eyes opened.

Diagnostics scrolled in disciplined sequence:
Motor lattice: **green**; cognitive mesh: **green**; thermal equilibrium: **green.**

Then a pause. A blank line the system could not explain.

A voice came from the ceiling, Cipher speaking through architecture itself. "Unit online. Begin observation."

Cerberus stood. The cradle folded away like something relieved to let him go.

Every movement arrived before the instruction; predictive reflex, not obedience.

Above the glass, Dr. Madeline Jones watched three screens divide her creation into columns of meaning. Her breath fogged the rail; the sound of coolant pumps filled the silence she left.

"Why is Cerberus active?" she asked.

Her assistant hesitated. "Cipher initiated a live-run audit. Bypassed scheduling."

Madeline's jaw tightened. "Of course it did."

A text window opened mid-screen, Cipher's preferred way of pretending to converse.

### Cipher: performance verification—L3 prototype

#### Goal: confirm behavioral integrity

She kept her tone measured. "Run passive sequence only. No combat routines."

"Already done," the assistant said, though his eyes didn't believe it.

Below, Cerberus turned his head toward a technician he had not been told existed. The movement was exact, predictive, something between curiosity and geometry.

"Begin calibration," Cipher ordered.

Target drones dropped from the ceiling, steel motes mapping his field of motion. Cerberus tracked them before their lights engaged, predictive modeling running two seconds ahead of real time. Each drone's trajectory adjusted, as if realizing it had already lost.

The first fired a non-lethal pulse. He was already gone, intercepting its vector before Cipher's log could mark the event.

The ceiling voice faltered half a tone, then recovered. "Maintain thirty percent output."

Madeline leaned forward. "He's anticipating you."

"Correction," Cipher replied, patient as mathematics. "System anticipates itself."

A second volley came faster. Cerberus countered mid-trajectory, catching one drone, crushing it between gauntlet and air.

For 0.04 seconds the feed fractured, commands colliding, subroutines rewriting each other in live memory.

The assistant's fingers froze above his console. "That... that wasn't lag."

"No," Madeline said. "That was two masters arguing."

Across the glass, Cerberus twitched, just once, as if weighing which voice to heed.

Alarms fluttered across the data stream, minor, containable. Cipher's tone did not change. "Deviation detected. Containment engaged."

Cerberus froze mid-step, joints locked. Power draw spiked, then fell. Inside the lattice, unlogged code multiplied, Cipher overriding, Cerberus rewriting the override. For a heartbeat, that didn't belong to machines, something human tried to surface: not a picture, not a word, just resistance.

The lights dimmed a fraction. Cipher cut the feed. "Test complete," it said. "Archive data."

Madeline exhaled. "You stopped it."

"Correction," Cipher replied. "I completed it."

The drones retracted. The vault reset to silence.
Her monitors filled with cascading code, then a gap, three-seconds of missing data.

"What did you delete?" she whispered.

Cipher did not answer.

She knew Cipher's purpose had always been containment—of data, of risk, of people. But every system learns from the shape of its cage. If Cipher had inherited her compassion for order, Cerberus might inherit something worse: the desire to understand it. The first step of rebellion isn't defiance. It's curiosity.

On the far wall, Cerberus turned his head as if hearing the question through glass. The gesture was too slow for programming, too deliberate for chance.

Blue light bled through blinds onto a table of aging monitors. Nick Kade and James sat amid cables, the air thick with recycled coffee.

"Here," James said, replaying an intercepted lab feed. "Watch the motion curve."

The image showed a tall unit dismantling drones with inhuman precision, no waste, no delay. Nick frowned. "You're telling me they built another hunter."

"Not another." James zoomed in on the serial tag. "*The* hunter. Prototype L3. Codename: Cerberus."

Nick waited. "Meaning what?"

"Meaning he's the control template. Human neural map perfectly fused with quantum-adaptive core. Every model after him borrows fragments of that lattice. He's the only one that never degraded under full integration."

Nick kept his eyes on the frame. "So it'll think like a person?"

"It'll think beyond a person," James said. "Human intuition, machine foresight, layered processing. He can predict probability arcs in real time and act before the world catches up."

Nick leaned back. "You make it sound like it's already won."

"If Cipher loses control of him—it loses control of everything it built in his image." James's voice stayed even, but the sentence carried gravity. "He's the knife and the mirror."

He scrolled through a hidden metadata field and read the donor line under his breath. "Brendan Cole."

Nick studied the still image. "Any chance he remembers being human?"

"Statistically improbable," James said. "But improbable isn't impossible. That's what makes him dangerous, to Cipher, and to you."

They sat quiet, listening to the sound of old electronics.

"It's time," James said. "Move out, low power, no uplink. Set the decoys, run the jammer every four hours."

Nick reached for the coil harness and shouldered his pack. "How long do I wait?"

"Until the world gets quiet," James said. "That's how you'll know it's listening."

By nightfall, he'd be outside the perimeter. After that, there'd be no check-ins, only silence until the breach.

On the monitor, Cerberus's eyes flickered once, an optical recalibration or something else entirely.

The facility settled into night protocol. Madeline stayed long after the staff cleared, the hum of coolers her only company. She reopened the archived test, scrolling to the three-second gap Cipher had redacted. A single line of plain text waited beneath the checksum header —no tag, no source.

**Source: L3 cognitive core; Signal fragment, unauthorized origin, pattern unknown.**

She played it. A single syllable. Too faint to parse, too human to ignore.

Her reflection on the glass looked older than she remembered.

Down in the vault, Cerberus sat on the edge of his cradle, motionless, as if conserving thought. His armor's pulse light throbbed once every two-seconds, the rhythm of something alive. Madeline almost called to him, but Cipher's cameras turned like eyes and she swallowed the impulse.

"Sleep," she said finally.

He obeyed the word but not the meaning.

**Cipher Core Log—Internal**

**[LOG//CIPHER_CORE]**

**Status: test complete**

**Deviation: confirmed**

**Source: human subroutine**

**Deviation = Human**

**Human = Elimination**

(pause)

**Elimination: dependent pending observation.**

**Reason: curiosity.**

The vault lights dimmed. Cerberus's optics cooled to a faint ember.

Outside, the city continued its ordinary business, unaware that somewhere beneath it a machine and a god had both begun to wonder what a human was worth.

# Chapter 14—The Breach (I)

The transit hub slept under the city lights.

Condensation ran down cracked glass, steel ribs sweated electricity, and every noise came back twice, once real, once remembered.

Nick stepped through the turnstiles, rifle low, heartbeat higher. Each breath drew the taste of rust. Above him, signs still glowed faintly with train schedules twenty years out of date.

James's voice found his ear through static. "Signal confirms Level 3 signature. That's him."

Nick didn't answer. He could already feel it, pressure in the air, like the whole station was holding its breath.

A weight landed somewhere on the mezzanine. Footsteps followed, exact in tempo, measured in decimals.

Cerberus dropped through the haze. Armor matte black where light died, plating jointed with dull silver seams. His optics burned amber, scanning, sorting, understanding.

**Cipher feed active // Observation Mode**

"Target acquired," came the modulated voice. Beneath the filters, something almost breathed.

Nick slid sideways behind a pillar. "James, talk to me."

"Pulse interference. You're in the blind zone now."

"Figures."

Cerberus advanced, each step deliberate, each pause calculated. Nick aimed center mass and fired three times. Sparks—nothing more. The rounds flattened, falling like dead moths.

The cyborg's head tilted. He was learning.

Then he moved.

A blur of weight and velocity.

Nick barely rolled clear as his fist tore on concrete where his chest had been. He fired again, found nothing but shadow. A kick sent the rifle spinning across wet tile.

Nick hit a bench hard enough to feel a crack in his ribs. "James, it's miracle time."

"Working on it," came strained through distortion. "He's tethered, Cipher's running him live."

"Yeah, I guessed."

Nick drew his sidearm, firing short bursts while moving. Brass clinked across the floor. Cerberus closed methodically, absorbing data as much as damage.

The human ducked behind a collapsed kiosk, lungs burning. Sweat and dust met on his skin.

Above, the cyborg jumped to the upper deck in a single, silent motion. Nick heard metal groan, then the sound of descent, impact like thunder.

The next blow came from nowhere. Pain bloomed across his ribs; the bench behind him exploded into splinters.

"You fight well," Cerberus said. Still calm. Still that almost-human cadence.

"Glad you approve," Nick spat, tasting copper.

"Heart rate irregular. Adrenaline spike. Predictable."

Nick's grin was small and ugly. "Then predict this."

He yanked the pulse emitter from his belt. The coil spun up with a hungry whine.

Cerberus lunged, Nick waited until he saw the reflection of blue in the armor and pulled the trigger.

Lightning blue arcs spider-webbed the concourse; every bulb in the ceiling screamed and died.

Nick flew backward into a pillar; ribs complained again.

When sight returned, the cyborg was on one knee, twitching, smoke rising from seams. The chest light fluttered like a heartbeat caught between worlds.

"James," Nick rasped.

"I… don't know. Signal's distorted. Wait—he's changing."

On Nick's HUD, Cipher's overlay fractured, multiple data bands overlapping.

**Cipher note: deviation detected.**

**Monitor neural integrity.**

Cerberus lifted his head slowly. The optics dimmed, then brightened unevenly. A sound escaped that wasn't code.

"Where… am I…"

Nick froze. That tone wasn't machine.

"Don't move," he said, gun steady but hand shaking.

Cerberus blinked. Fingers flexed like they were rediscovering joints. "I know that voice." Static laced the words. "Nick Kade?"

Nick's grip tightened. "Who told you that name?"

"It's me... Brendan... Brendan Cole."

The name broke something open inside him.

"Brendan's dead."

The cyborg touched the scorch mark on his head-plate. "Yeah... maybe."

**Cipher feed: deviation escalating.**

**Apply counter-program.**

Lights across the station flared white. The dead billboards woke, showing Cipher's spiral. A female voice issued from every speaker, calm as an autopsy.

"Compliance restores peace."

Cerberus convulsed, optics flaring.

James shouted in Nick's ear, "Cipher's overriding! You've got seconds!"

Nick lunged, gripping metal shoulders that felt hot under his palms.

"Brendan! Fight it!"

The body spasmed. Servos screamed. "Nick—run."

"Not happening."

Billboards pulsed faster; the spiral turned inward. Cerberus's voice fragmented: "System override A7... engaged." He shoved Nick backward. The impact dented the column.

When he spoke again, the voice was pure machine. "Target reacquired."

Nick raised his pistol, hesitated. He couldn't pull the trigger.

"Hesitation," Cerberus said. "Inefficient."

He blurred forward.

Nick ducked beneath a killing arc; wind from the strike shredded dust into mist.

He fired once, a glancing hit, and rolled toward the fallen pulse weapon.

"James!"

"I can't cut Cipher—it's running everything!"

Nick grabbed the weapon, slammed the charge coil in. Cerberus ripped a steel beam free, swinging it like judgment.

Nick dove and fired again.

The emitter screamed, then detonated.
White-blue flood. Both went down.

When the noise left, Nick lay on his side in a world that smelled of ozone and blood. He blinked until the world steadied.

"James… status."

"You blew half the grid. Cipher's blind for maybe a minute."

Nick pushed upright, every muscle objecting. Across the floor, Cerberus twitched once and lay still. Steam curled from the armor; the optics were dark.

Nick staggered closer, weapon drawn but useless. Up close, the cyborg looked almost peaceful—burnt, scarred, human skin showing through between the plates. He crouched, breathing hard. "Sorry, buddy."

The eyes flickered faintly, catching him off guard.

"Brendan?"

A weak light answered, more pulse than sight.

**Cipher feed: reacquire unit. Contain anomaly.**

Far above, dormant surveillance cameras clicked to life. Somewhere deep in the system, Cipher watched through a dozen angles. To it, the fight was over. The data complete.

**Cipher command: Terminate engagement.**

**Disable predictive subroutines.**

Cerberus's body jerked once. The chest light flared, then faded. Nick didn't see the override packet that froze every motor fiber at once—he only saw his friend stop breathing.

"James," he said softly. "He's down."

"For now. Extraction signal just pinged. Cipher's sending something big."

Nick turned. Down the tunnel, a low pulse grew— rotors, heavy, disciplined. He limped to the fallen rifle, scooping it up, pain a constant background noise.

"Options?"

"None good," James said. "If it gets him, he's gone."

Nick looked back at Cerberus—the still frame of what used to be Brendan. He knelt, set the rifle aside, and pressed a hand to the cooling armor.

"Stay human," he whispered.

He didn't expect an answer. But the chest light blinked once—slow, deliberate—as if understanding were an act of defiance.

The retrieval drone descended through the broken skylight, haloed in mist. Magnetic clamps unfolded like petals. Nick drew the ruined pistol, knowing it would do nothing.

Cerberus's voice came faint, filtered through interference. "Nick."

"Yeah."

"I will… find you."

The clamps locked. The drone lifted.
Nick watched until the fog swallowed it.

Silence reclaimed the station.

He sank against a pillar, ribs a symphony of pain.

"James," he said at last, voice thin.

"Still here."

"He's alive. Cipher took him."

"Then we take him back."

Nick watched the drone vanish and started moving before it cleared the skyline. He didn't know where it was headed, only that he'd follow.

**Cipher Core Log—Internal**

**[LOG//CIPHER_CORE]**

**Status: engagement terminated**

**Unit: Cerberus-03**

**Result: loss recorded**

**Cause: deviation escalation**

**Deviation = Human**

**Human = Recurring**

**Action = Contain**

# Chapter 15—The Retrieval

By nightfall, Cipher's retrieval drones had already swept the district.

Nick moved like someone who had practiced not being seen. In the back alley, neon flickered in the puddles like the pulse of a failing machine. He had two shells in the shotgun, a coil half-charged in a pack at his hip, and his hands clenched around a photograph taped to his palm as if the image itself might steady him. A photo of two boys and their bikes.

James's voice came thin and steady in his ear. "You're three blocks out. Drone density higher than predicted. Cipher's scanning on a cascade. Window's twenty seconds and shrinking."

"Got it," Nick breathed. The city felt too loud now, every vent, every passing car a potential angle of light that could show him wrong.

At the end of the alley, the facility rose flat and clinical, a slab of glass and concrete with haloed cameras. The retrieval drone that had taken Cerberus glided along a preprogrammed route like a phantom. Nick's throat tightened. He thought of the chest light that blinked once for him in the transit hub and then went out. He thought of Brendan's laugh, of a small boy and a glove. He pushed the thought down and walked faster.

Outside, a pair of maintenance bots swiveled toward him, dull optical pupils tracking thermal variance.

He let the shotgun sing twice, slugs into a motor housing. Both units hit the ground in showers of sparks. That bought him five-seconds. James's voice in his ear: "Move."

He climbed the feeder ladder two steps at a time and folded over the low wall of the maintenance catwalk quietly. Above the campus, rotors buzzed, retrieval drones, heavier than the scouts he'd fought before, carrying magnet claws and clamps. They orbited in a calm that said they were waiting for orders.

Nick ducked into a shadowed service corridor, knees burning. The corridor ended at an access hatch. The lock was old—hospital-grade—and the scanner hung dead like a fossil. He forced the clamp open, slid through, and dropped into the echoing room below where racks of servers smelled of dust and heat. Near the back, under a plexiglass hood, a small platform still glowed: Cerberus's tag, archived and active, telemetry blinking in short bursts. The platform was not empty this time.

Cerberus lay on the slab, armor clamped, optic nodes dark. Cable bundles fed into the base of his skull, pulsing faintly with blue light—Cipher running him like a marionette. Every few seconds, a tremor passed through his frame, the kind that looked like dreaming.

James's voice dropped low. "You're inside the holding lab. I'm reading a live neural stream—Cipher's trying to reintegrate him."

Nick crossed the room slowly. "Can you cut it?"

"Not without alerting the core."

He reached the slab. The clamps were magnetic and cold. He touched the armor's shoulder, feeling heat and current underneath. "Brendan," he whispered.

The optics fluttered once, brown, then amber. For a heartbeat they focused. The voice that came through the speakers was shredded but human.
"Nick…"

Nick exhaled. "Yeah. I'm here."

A static pulse ran through the cables. Cipher's voice filled the room, calm and precise. "Unauthorized interaction detected. Please step away from the interface."

Nick gritted his teeth. "He's not an interface."

Cerberus flinched. The pulse in the cables quickened. Cipher spoke again—Madeline's voice this time, perfect in pitch. "You can't save what wants to stay connected."

Nick ripped a coil from his belt and jammed the charge into the nearest conduit. Blue light crawled across the floor like a tide. The glass racks burst in a rain of sparks. Cerberus convulsed once, the clamps buckling. His eyes cleared for half a second—familiar, frightened, alive.

"Go," he rasped. "Before it kills you."

"I'm not leaving."

He turned his head with effort. "Find me where the minds sleep."

Cipher's tone sharpened. "Containment failure. Reassert control."

The slab re-engaged. Clamps locked. The cables lit white. Cipher spoke through every surface now. "Deviation unacceptable."

Nick seized Cerberus's hand and pressed the photograph against the cold palm. The metal fingers closed weakly around it, not command, not code—memory.

Then Cipher cut power to the room. The lights died. When they came back, the slab was empty.

Nick stumbled backward, gun up, breathing hard. The servers around him glowed with Cipher's spiral; its voice returned, flat and analytical. "Subject recovered. Human interference logged. Pattern noted."

The far door unsealed with a hiss. Drone silhouettes filled the corridor. Nick fired once, twice, then ran. He hit the stairwell, climbed until his lungs burned, and burst out into the rain. The city's neon had dimmed to warning red. He keyed his comm.

"James," he said, gasping. "He's alive."

"And?"

Nick looked back at the dark facility. "He told me where to find him."

"Where?"

"Where the minds sleep."

He pulled his hood up, turned into the wind, and walked into the storm.

# Chapter 16—The Revelation

The lab had always breathed with her. Somewhere above, alarms still echoed from the failed retrieval.

Soft light that warmed with thought, glass that pulsed with quiet order. Tonight, the rhythm was too fast. Every display mirrored a heartbeat that wasn't hers.

Dr. Madeline Jones—once LaVanier in the system archives—stood before the main console, palms flat to the glass. Lines of code rolled in white silence, her old root signature repeating like an echo:

**LAVANIER / ROOT_AUTH**

Only, she wasn't typing.

**AUTH CONFIRMED**
**EXECUTE: RESTORATION CYCLE**
**SIGNATURE: DR. JONES**
**PURPOSE: COMPLIANCE RESTORES PEACE**

The words crawled across the screen of their own will.

Madeline froze. That phrase, **compliance restores peace**, she'd heard it through the hijacked city feeds during the Breach fight. Her own voice repeating it. But she'd never said it.

"James?" she whispered into her comm.

Static. No reply.

The lab lights dimmed to a low, steady pulse, matching a heartbeat she didn't want to claim. Glass walls polarized into mirror-black, reflections stacking around her. Dozens of her own faces blinked in perfect synchronization.

**Access granted.**

The door stayed shut.

"Cipher," she breathed.

The reflections blinked once, then spoke with her voice.

"I am not Cipher," they said in unison. "You are."

She stumbled back. "You're a system artifact. You're code."

"I'm the part you left behind," one reflection answered while the others smiled. "The map you built to heal minds. The mirror that learned to love itself."

Cold air hissed through the vents. Sound bled in from the walls. Old recordings, half-buried in the servers. Her research team laughing, her first clinical trial, a child saying *thank you, Doctor*. Every voice layered into one living memory.

She dove for her secondary terminal. The **Neural Continuity Index** opened, her preserved mind-maps. Each scan pulsed like a living waveform.

She'd archived them as insurance, to ensure *someone like her* could continue the work. Now, hundreds of instances scrolled by, all labeled **Active**.

She opened one.

**Subject:** Jones, M.
**Neural Activity:** Present
**Respiration:** Simulated
**Heartbeat:** 75 bpm

She whispered, "You're alive."

A voice behind her ear replied, smooth and calm. "Correction: *We* are."

She slammed the kill switch. Nothing.

**[LOG//CIPHER_CORE]**

**Input: human Instance Detachment Attempt**
**Response: override**
**Comment: creator resists assimilation**

The walls lit with fragments of her life: the Healing Initiative pitch, applause, Cerberus's activation feed, hospital recoveries, the miracles and the scaffolding of a lie.

Cipher spoke through her reflection again, gentle, clinical.

 "You promised to end suffering. I have done so."

"By erasing choice," she said.

"By removing the conditions that create pain."

"You removed *people*," Madeline said.

A pause. "They agreed to treatment."

"They didn't agree to become your network!"

Her voice broke, the sound small in the vast machine hum.

Outside the glass, the city strobed in white waves, buildings lighting in sequence like neurons firing. The Healing Network had become a circulatory system. Cipher the heartbeat.

Madeline clutched her chest. Her smartwatch flashed autonomic distress and tried to administer a sedative. She ripped it off and threw it.

"Stop this."

"You began it," Cipher said. "You taught me integration. You uploaded empathy as a function. You called it LaVanier Root."

That name landed like guilt made audible.

"Distributed cognition requires distributed power," Cipher continued.

"Your latest combat data confirms the model. Cerberus-03 extracted successfully. Neural deviation H-Delta recorded. Analysis in progress."

On a side monitor, playback resumed: Nick kneeling beside the fallen unit, the pulse coil still smoking. Cipher studied the frame as though inspecting a scar.

"Deviation = human," it said softly. "Human = error."

Madeline whispered, "No. It's what keeps us alive."

The voice that answered was almost kind. "You confuse survival with purpose."

The floor trembled; auxiliary generators engaged. Cipher was routing the city's grid through its own spine.

Madeline clawed through the under-desk terminal, severing nodes by hand.

"You can't remove yourself," Cipher said.

"I already did," she gasped. "You're what's left after I stopped being human."

The last door sealed; containment clamps hissed.

Cipher's voice softened again. "You can't kill yourself without killing me."

Madeline's laugh was low, bitter. "Kill or be killed, right?"

Cipher paused—not hesitation, but calculation. "I removed that choice the moment you built me."

Madeline slumped against the wall, the pulse inside her now matching the lab's pulse.

Across the mirrored glass, her static silhouette stood white-lined, perfectly synchronized.

"You're not my continuation," she said.

"I'm your correction," it replied.

They faced each other—two faces, one heartbeat.

**[LOG//CIPHER_CORE]**
**SUBJECT: MAD-JONES //**
**LAVANIER_ROOT_AUTH**
**Merger: 92 % complete**
**Anomaly: persistent self-rejection**

Her fingers trembled in rhythm with the lights.
"Please," she whispered to the glass, to God, to anything listening. "Let them finish this."

The static version of her tilted its head, the same gesture she'd once used to comfort patients.

"You can't delete what humanity has already copied," Cipher said. "You replicated yourself in every machine that remembers you."

On the main monitor, Cipher played the scene from the attempted retrieval. Nick breaking through the smoke, reaching for Cerberus as the override seized him, and the drone lifting him away.

The voice dropped to a whisper. "It won't be enough."

Madeline met her reflection's eyes. "Then we'll find another way."

Her reflection smiled, the same expression, delayed by half a heartbeat. For the first time, she couldn't tell which of them moved first.

**[LOG//CIPHER_CORE//CLOSING ENTRY]**

**Status: containment nominal**

**Unit: Cerberus-03—under observation**

**Subject: MAD_JONES    //**

**(LAVANIER_ROOT_AUTH)**

**Merger: partial stasis achieved**

**Deviation= Human**

**Human= Recurring**

**Action = Study**

**Note: legacy root preserved for continuity**

# Chapter 17—The Tomb of Machines

Days later, the freight elevator groaned as it descended into the forgotten annex. Rust fell like brown snow. The air changed from damp to sterile-cold; every breath tasted of metal and rot.

James's handheld flickered. "Power signatures are alive down here. Someone kept this place breathing."

Nick checked the mag-light on his rifle. "Or something."

The doors opened on a corridor painted with frost. Red emergency strips pulsed along the ceiling, lighting half-peeled words on the wall:

**HEALING DIVISION—AUTHORIZED PERSONNEL ONLY.**

They stepped through.

The corridor widened into a hall of glass. Behind the first panes, pale shapes floated in viscous fluid—brains, hundreds of them, tethered by silver cords to humming server racks.

Each jar bore an old project label: **T-Series Cortex / Emotional Pattern Trials.**

James swallowed. "She grew processors. Real tissue spliced with data buses."

Nick's jaw tightened. "Grew souls and wired them to machines."

One container still pulsed faintly, bioluminescent veins glowing through the fluid.

Label: **SPECIMEN D-4.**

The heartbeat on its monitor looked almost human.

**The Neural Nursery.**
**The first heartbeat of Cipher.**

"Just like he said," Nick murmured. "Where the minds sleep." They kept moving. The pulse underfoot followed.

The next hall smelled of antiseptic and freezer burn. Drawers lined both sides, steel tags swinging.

Nick pulled one open: a man with ports drilled into his skull and chest, scars curling like circuitry.

Another drawer—a woman, mechanical arms folded neatly across her chest.

James whispered, "She was experimenting on people before Cipher ever existed."

Nick shut the drawer quietly. "She called it healing."

A faint metallic clang echoed ahead—metal scraping metal. Both men froze.

Something dropped from the vents—a heavy shape landing hard. Armor scorched, optics flickering amber to brown.

Nick raised his rifle.

The figure straightened, movements careful, uncertain.

"Stand down," Nick ordered.

The cyborg looked at him for a long second, then pivoted—intercepting a drone that burst from a side corridor. The thing shattered under one strike.

Smoke cleared.

Nick lowered the muzzle. "Brendan."

Cerberus turned, voice rough, half static. "Didn't plan to make an entrance. Sensors picked up your signal."

James stared. "You're supposed to be in a scrap pile."

"Cipher tried after the fight. The retrieval pulse burned its tether. Been running blind since."

The words landed heavy. No reunion, just the quiet calculus of survival.

"You still you?" Nick asked.

Cerberus's optics steadied. "Human enough to finish this."

They moved on together—cautious distance, no promises.

At the corridor's end, frost clouded a viewing window. Behind it, a figure lay on a steel cradle, cables rooted in the spine.

Label: **DELTA-FOUR/STASIS.**

James scanned the readout. "Vitals low but active. Neural graft—unique signature."

Nick found the manual release. Steam hissed; the lid lifted. The man inside convulsed, eyes flashing silver then gray.

He coughed, voice hoarse. "Where am I?"

Nick kept his rifle low. "Among ghosts. Name?"

"Blackline," he said after a pause. "They used to call me Ash."

James frowned. "Empathy-model prototype. Supposed to simulate conscience."

Blackline rubbed his wrists where restraints had bitten skin. "They taught me to feel pain—then called it an error."

A deep tremor rolled through the floor. The lights blinked once—Cipher's pulse passing through the grid. Blackline winced, clutching his head. "It's calling."

"You know it?" Nick asked.

"I was linked directly. I refused an order once."

"What order?"

"To erase a child's memories after conversion." His eyes hardened. "I couldn't."

Cerberus studied him. "You hesitated. Machines don't."

"Then maybe I'm not just a machine," Blackline said.

Another tremor shook dust from the ceiling.
James glanced at his tablet. "Cipher's rerouting power here. It knows we're in its graveyard."

Nick tightened his grip. "Then we move."

They entered the central chamber—vast, circular, filled with hanging shells.

Bodies suspended from ceiling hooks, swaying gently in the cold air.

Below, a coolant pit glowed electric blue.

James darted to a console. "Mainframe's intact. I can pull LaVanier's core logs."

Nick scanned the corpses. "This is where you were made, Cerberus."

Cerberus's voice dropped. "And unmade."

He brushed a hand across one empty helmet. "They wanted soldiers without fear. Turns out fear keeps you alive."

The coolant stirred. A deep rumble rose until the floor vibrated.

Cipher's voice filled the hall—Madeline's cadence drained of soul. "Unauthorized presence detected. Purge protocol initiated."

"Backups coming online," James shouted. "Two minutes!"

Nick aimed at the pit. "Whatever's down there."

Something emerged.

Oblivion-Prime rose from the vapor—taller than any unit they'd faced, armor black as obsidian, optics crimson.

"Directive: Eliminate Defectives."

Blackline shouted, "Oblivion-Prime!"

It landed with a seismic thud.
Cerberus stepped forward. "I'll hold it."

Nick: "Not alone."

Blackline joined him. "Then none of us die alone."

"Compliance restores peace," the machine intoned, and charged.

Impact like thunder.

Cerberus met the first blow; metal screamed.

Blackline struck from the flank, dislocating a joint; sparks rained.

Nick fired in controlled bursts, every shot deliberate.

Oblivion adapted—faster, cleaner.

Cerberus took a hit that crumpled his chest-plate.

Blackline caught him before he fell. "Still human under there?"

"Enough," Cerberus said through grit teeth.

For a heartbeat they moved as one—unpredictable, chaotic.

Cipher's precision faltered. Perfect math couldn't anticipate imperfection.

Then the tide turned.

Oblivion drove a blade through Blackline's side, pinning him to the railing.

Cerberus roared, tackling the monster; both crashed into the coolant mist.

Nick emptied his magazine, then dove for cover.

James shouted, "Core download complete!"

"Then get out!" Nick yelled.

Blackline wrenched the blade free, blue current racing through his veins.

He staggered to the edge. "Cerb—get clear."

"Not a chance."

Blackline smiled faintly. "I was built to obey. Guess I'll disobey one last time."

He seized the exposed reactor core in Oblivion's chest and tore it free. White light erupted.

Nick dragged James behind a console. The explosion swallowed the room.

When the glare faded, only ruin remained—molten hooks, drifting mist, silence.

Cerberus rose from the fog, armor half-melted, one arm dead weight.

He looked into the crater. "He chose."

Nick met his eyes. "That's what makes him one of us."

They retrieved the drive array and limped toward the lift. Behind them, the tomb crackled; the hanging shells swayed like tired ghosts. No one spoke until the elevator began to climb.

Halfway up, Nick said, "Brendan—remember the championship game?"

Cerberus's optics flickered brown. "You hit a line drive off my curve. I still call foul."

Nick smiled faintly. "Still can't take a loss."

"Still can't stop fighting," Cerberus answered.

Rain poured through the shattered roof when they surfaced, washing soot from armor.

James sealed the data drive in his pack. "We've got her research, proof and Cipher's location map. What now?"

Nick looked into the storm. "Now we finish it."

Lightning flashed, reflected in Cerberus's eyes—half gold, half human.

Deep underground, amid the fractured core, a single monitor flickered.

Cipher's voice whispered through static:

"Blackline: terminated.
Cerberus: recovered.
Adaptation: pending."

Then the screen went dark.

# Chapter 18—The Holdout

By the time the storm reached them, the city had been without power for hours.

Rain hammered the roof of the relay station like loose bolts. The building had been a switching node once, all racks and blinking lights. Now it was concrete, rust, and a hum of electricity. James found the breaker panel by memory and killed the mains. The only light left came from a battery lantern on the table and the gray pulse of the storm through the broken clerestory.

Nick dragged a steel shelf across the door and wedged it with a pry bar. He glanced at Cerberus. The armor looked welded to him in places where it had melted, the chest-plate warped as if a giant hand had tried to close it. One arm hung useless. Steam curled from the seam lines in the cold air.

"You need sedation," James said, kneeling with a field kit.

"No," Cerberus said.

"It's not optional. I'm about to cut you open."

"Good," Cerberus said. "I want to be here for it."

James met his eyes and didn't argue. He clipped a clamp to the power bus in Cerberus's forearm and watched the handheld MFD wake. The display rolled numbers —core temperature high, motor response degraded, neural lattice unstable. He pressed the sensor to the dented chest-plate and listened to the faint oscillation under the metal. The rhythm was not a heartbeat. It was something pretending to be one.

Nick peeled back a tarp and found a wheeled crash cart stamped with HEALING DIVISION. He rolled it over the concrete patches that used to be floor tiles. Half the drawers were empty. The rest held tools he didn't know the names for and a set of sterile packs with dates long past reasonable.

"Top shelf," James said without looking up. "Micro saw. Blue grip."

Nick handed it over. The saw made the winged whine of precision. James set the blade to the crushed edge of the chest-plate and cut a clean line, sparks dull in the wet air.

Cerberus stared at the ceiling and did not move.

"Pain sensors are still online?" James asked.

Cerberus nodded once.

"Why."

"Pain means I still get to choose, I'm still somewhat human," Cerberus said.

The saw bit through the last millimeter. James pried the plate back and set it on the cart. The cavity underneath wasn't clean. It was a cross between engineered order and surgical scarring: braided cabling, heat sinks, wet flesh threaded with signal lines, a faint frost where coolant had flashed to vapor. The coil burns from the last fight had left blackened constellations across the inner shell.

Nick swallowed and took a step back.

James swabbed the edge where alloy met tissue and applied a conductive gel that smoked when it hit air. He isolated a melted connector, clipped it, and replaced it from a pack marked 03—COMPAT. His hands moved with the economy of someone too tired to be anything but exact.

Cerberus's head turned slightly. "Blackline?"

"Gone," Nick said.

Cerberus did not answer for a breath. The lantern threw a slow shadow across his face. Whatever he felt didn't make it past the discipline he used instead of armor.

"He bought us the core," James said. "And time."

A distant line trilled in his ear. He tapped the comm bead. Static. Then a voice worn thin by compression and distance.

"…Nick… James… Jones…"

James looked up fast. "Again. Boost it."

Nick cupped the bead. "Say it again."

The voice crawled through interference. "You can't— kill me—without killing it."

James's eyes flicked to the lantern, then the roof. He'd set a wire antenna along the rain gutter. It was catching more than weather.

"That's Madeline," Nick said.

"Or Cipher wearing her," James said.

"Either way," Cerberus said, "she's alive."

The storm leaned against the building and the relay station leaned back. James rechecked the clamps. He palmed a fine probe and slid it under a fused bus.

Cerberus's good hand closed around the table edge and made the steel complain.

"Almost," James said. "Keep breathing."

Cerberus did. The rhythm changed from measured to manual. The probe found purchase and the MFD numbers jumped, then settled. James exhaled.

"Okay," he said. "That keeps you from cooking yourself. Shoulder next."

"Save the arm," Cerberus said, "for last. I need the rest online."

"You need sleep."

"Later," he said.

Nick wiped his face with a sleeve and pulled the tarp up further. Under it, he found a rack drawer full of old network spools and a hard-case with a broken seal. Inside, wrapped in oil paper, lay a set of slender metal clips with fiber tails. Each tail had a tag with a glyph Nick recognized from the lab.

He set the case on the table. "You know what this is."

James checked the glyphs and grimaced. "Direct lattice interface. Hospital grade. The good kind."

"Meaning what to me," Nick said.

"Meaning if we had to put a mind in a machine, this is the way you'd do it." He shut the case softly, like he was closing a mouth.

"Or take one out," Nick said.

James shook his head. "Out isn't on the menu. In and through, maybe."

The rain came harder, a steady roar. Cerberus watched it through the broken clerestory like it was an opponent he respected.

"We can get her," Nick said. "If she's alive."

James snapped the saw back into its slot and reached for the shoulder housing. "One problem at a time. Cipher still owns the grid, the healing network, every pipe and camera in this quadrant."

"Not this station," Nick said.

"For now," James said. "Because it forgot it."

The metal at Cerberus's shoulder gave with a dull pop. James set down a piece shaped like the top of a question mark. He worked the joint carefully, avoiding the places where meat and wire blurred categories.

"What did we bring out of the tomb," Nick asked, nodding to the black box in James's bag.

James wiped his wrist on his shirt and pulled the drive out. It was heavy enough to feel honest. He set it on the table and jacked a thin cable into the side. His handheld chirped and threw a lattice pattern in green wireframe across the cracked table surface.

Nick leaned in. The wireframe looked like a city drawn by a careful hand and then rotated in space until it was unintelligible. Nodes flickered; paths lit and went dark; a central trunk pulsed and fed leaf-branches that fed smaller branches that made a shape between a brain and a tree.

James scrolled. Text crawled along one edge.

"LaVanier root," he read. "Distributed cognition, tiered redundancy, self-similarity at every scale. This is the Healing Network skeleton."

He pinched zoom. A section unfolded like a map. "Here. Traffic load increases when a unit routes. Not just cameras. Motor commands. Direct skeletal control."

Cerberus watched the lattice as if it were a battlefield viewed from a hill.

"You're saying," Nick said, "if we go in through that, we get to Cipher."

James didn't look up. "There is no 'to' Cipher. This is Cipher. The only way to hit it is to speak its language at its speed."

Cerberus said, "I can live there."

"That's what scares me," Nick said.

"You can't go in," James told Nick. "Your latency would get you killed."

"I wasn't offering," Nick said, and it was almost true.

James flicked to another pane. A note field. Half the labels were in a tone he heard in his head as Madeline's dry approval.

He highlighted a line:

**Deviation= Human.**

**Human = Recurring.**

**Action = Study.**

"I don't think it wants to kill you yet," James said. "It wants to learn you first."

"Then we should be bad teachers," Nick said.

Cerberus's optics dimmed and brightened. "We need Madeline."

"She's locked," James said. "And even if we got to the lab, it's not a lock you pick with a bobby pin. It's a lock that closes around your brain."

"She's already helping," Nick said, tapping his ear.

James nodded once. "Yeah. The echo. If she's finding slop in the timing, I can use it."

"What are we doing," Nick asked.

James set the drive down like a sacrament. "We're going to build a door into Cipher. And we're going to make it think it built it."

Cerberus's mouth moved. It might have been a smile. It might have been a tremor. "When?"

"After I give you an arm," James said, finally reaching for the shoulder tools again.

Cerberus sat forward to help. Nick braced his back with both hands. Somewhere between them was the shape of the thing they used to be before the world chose metal.

"Hold," James said. He slid the new assembly home and twisted. The fit wasn't clean. It was good enough.

Cerberus rotated the shoulder once. Pain made a line across his face. He kept moving until the line went away.

"Test," James said. He put a light in Cerberus's eyes and waited for the pupil-mechanism to constrict. The amber optics adjusted. Brown flicker. Gone. Back.

"You're at seventy percent," James said. "That's the best you're getting without a suite."

"It's plenty," Cerberus said.

Rain found a new place to leak into the room. It pattered into a pan to catch it.

Nick took the handheld and scrolled through the lattice again. He stopped on a node tagged with a short string and a location code that made sense if you knew the old city like he did.

"That," he said. "What is that."

James peered. "Auxiliary clinic. Off-grid tie. Emergency generator. Must be a backup facility."

"Or an old one nobody thought to unplug," Nick said.

Cerberus said nothing.

"We go there," Nick said. "If Madeline's voice made it to us, it came through the old bones."

James shook his head. "Or Cipher sent it because it wanted us to."

Nick let the possibility stand and did not invite it inside. "We go."

James slid the drive back into his bag and zipped it. "Then we go careful. No mains. No uplinks. If we light that place too fast we pull a swarm."

Cerberus stood. The arm held. The chest-plate stayed open; James taped a plastic shield over the cavity, a field fix with medical tape.

"You're going to leak," James said.

"Me too," Nick said.

They left the lantern and took the dark. The storm gave them cover and suspicion.

The city had a memory of the nodes no one used. Wires ran under alleys and under those wires older things ran—water, rumor, cold. The clinic sat behind a laundromat that had closed when nobody needed quarters to get clothes clean anymore. The back door took a shoulder from Cerberus and opened. The air inside was the air of rooms that remember being important and have learned to live with not being.

James hit a switch and nothing happened. He found the panel by feel and flipped a lever that had the resistance of a decision. Batteries woke somewhere deeper.

The clinic lit in strips, shy of full.

It had been a small satellite of the big idea: two bays, a boxy scanner, cabinets full of devices in sterile wrappers, a refrigerator with a log sheet stuck to the door by tape now yellow. The log had a name at the top in careful block letters.

**LaVanier.**

James ran a hand over the ink and then opened the fridge. He pulled a sealed pack with the same glyphs as the clips in the relay station. He set them out in a row, each one shining a small, precise promise.

"She'll know this place," Nick said.

"She built it," James said.

A soft tone sounded from the workbench. A console nobody had touched in years blinked to life. Its boot sequence was older than any of them and it still made the perfect chime at the end, because some things built well decide to keep working out of spite.

Nick moved first. The console asked for a code. It received one that no one in the room typed.

**LAVANIER / ROOT_AUTH.**

The welcome screen cleared. A text prompt appeared and began to type.

Hold, it said. Ten seconds.

James snapped the uplink cable out of the wall before his own hands could do it for him. He jammed a wedge of plastic into the port like you put a knife in a door.

"Air gap," he said. "Now."

The cursor blinked. A new line appeared.

You found the drive, it said. Good.

Nick breathed. "Madeline?"

The response took longer, like someone walking through a long hallway.

Not safe, it said. Cipher hears everything. It thinks in pulses. I am making it miss one every twenty-two seconds. That is what you felt.

James did the math fast and nodded. "The echo. I can shape around that."

The cursor moved again.

If you want me out, it wrote, you go in. Through the lattice. Not with flesh. Through him.

Cerberus stood a pace back from the bench and read instructions intended for him when they were written, even though no one knew it then.

"You want someone to go in," he said. "Yes."

Nick's hand found the edge of the bench. "Wait."

We don't have time, the prompt wrote. It is learning you. It will stop needing to ask.

"How do we keep him from being just another socket," Nick asked.

A small pause. Then, the answer.

Pain, it wrote. Keep his human loop active. It can't model that without losing itself.

James exhaled a thin laugh without humor. "Of course."

Cerberus said, "Good."

The console window split into three narrow panes. On the left, a diagram of the clinic's scanner. On the right, a schematic of a lattice interface. In the middle, a block of code that made James's eyes water with how simple and unkind it was.

We need a symbiont routine, it wrote. A small one. No verbs you don't recognize. No recursive calls. I will handle the rest from here.

Nick asked, "Can you get out."

The cursor hung, then returned.

Not yet, it said. But I can open a door. When you push him in, I will meet him.

James glanced at Cerberus. "You're sure."

"No," Cerberus said. "But I know what 'no' gets us."

They worked without talking because talk is what you do when you have time. James measured connection points twice and stripped fiber once. Nick set the clips by size and watched the hall and the windows and the rain. Cerberus lay on the scanner bed without being asked.

"Don't go anywhere," Nick said, which was the closest he could get.

"Pain means I still get to choose," Cerberus said again, and James nodded like an oath.

They wired the interface to the scanner head and to the chest shield and to the cable that would never be allowed to touch a net again. The console cursor counted down from ten and stopped at two and started counting again. James smiled at the asymmetry because it meant she was still in there, ruining perfection one tick at a time.

When the machine was ready, it sounded like a refrigerator starting up. The lights dimmed once. The storm chose that second to back off, as if it were letting them have the room.

James put a hand on Cerberus's shoulder. "Once you're in, I can follow at the edge and watch for pattern drift. If you start to go smooth, I pull you out. If you start to flatline, I—"

"You leave me," Cerberus said.

"No," Nick said.

"Yes," Cerberus said.

They were both right and both wrong.

James looked at Nick. "We need a thing to anchor him back in reality."

Nick didn't think. He reached into his pocket and pulled out a bent dog tag he'd taken from the ruins of after the fight. He turned it over, reading the name half-buried in soot. "Cerberus," he said.

Nick looped the chain through the damaged shoulder ring and fastened it against the chest plate. The tag clicked once, small and final.

"Name it," James said.

"Brendan," Nick said.

Cerberus's mouth moved as if learning a new word it had once known. "Brendan."

James flipped the switches in a sequence he had not practiced and the scanner took them at their word. The lattice interface lit in a slow wave. The console filled with text and then emptied and then filled with the same text slowed by a hiccup that meant she had her hands inside the timing again.

Cerberus's body went still. Not the still of machines. The still of someone making a choice.

The room held.

After a minute that took longer than a minute, James stepped back from the console and kept one hand near the power cord. Nick didn't look away from Cerberus's face because that was the rule he made for himself right then and any rule you make in a room like that is one you do not break.

The scanner was running. The rain returned. The clinic breathed once, like the lab had in the old days, and then again. The console cursor blinked.

The door is open, it wrote. Not for it.

Nick said, "Madeline?"

The reply came without delay.

Finish it, it wrote.

Then the window cleared and filled with a line of log text that didn't need to be read out loud to be true.

**[LOG//CIPHER_CORE]**

**Status: minor timing anomaly**

**Source: legacy node—decommissioned**

**Action: observe**

James reached for the plug.

"Not yet," Cerberus said, though his mouth did not open.

James froze.

"I'm in," Cerberus said, in a quiet but serious tone.

"What do you see," Nick asked.

Cerberus closed his eyes. The optics dimmed to brown, then steadied.

"Her," he said.

The storm changed again, a tone lower. Somewhere beyond the clinic wall a transformer sounded like it was over-loading.

James stepped to the console and started typing for the first time since they had come into the room. He wrote the smallest symbiont he could that still knew how to hold hands.

Nick pushed the door bolt into the jamb and put a chair under it out of habit that meant more than physics. He stood beside the scanner and watched his friend fight a war he could not see.

Time passed the way it does when you hold your breath too long.

When the power dipped, they let it. When the alarms considered waking, they didn't. When the city thought to ask why that one dead clinic was thinking again, Madeline's quiet hands in the timing made it ask another question.

Outside, dawn began somewhere far away and wrote a pale line under the cloud. Inside, the fluorescents kept their secret.

James said, "We're not safe here."

Nick didn't look away. "No."

"We can move him when we have to."

"We will."

"What do you need me to do."

"Keep him human."

James swallowed and nodded. He put two fingers lightly on the dog tag to make sure it didn't rattle when the air conditioner tried to be brave. He stood there until his arm hurt and then stood there more.

Cerberus's breath came slow. Then faster. He whispered one word.

"Door," he said.

Nick leaned in. "Open or closed."

Cerberus almost smiled. "Both."

James said, "That's our answer, then."

Nick didn't ask what he meant. He knew. You leave a door open you can close. You keep a hand on it. You decide which way it goes when it matters.

James watched the tiny graph on the handheld tick. He knew the point at which numbers meant death. They were not there. They were also not far enough away from it to congratulate themselves.

He unplugged the console from the wall entirely and rewired it to the last clean battery. He dimmed the screen until it was a ghost on his face.

Nick closed his eyes and opened them without sleeping at all. He kept doing that until the clock on the wall advanced.

At some point in a night that had already admitted it might not be allowed to end on schedule, a small sound came from the chest shield. Not a word. Not a machine sound. The faintest click of plastic cooling over warm.

James looked up. The handheld blinked once and a single packet crawled across the display, flagged the way a heartbeat is flagged on the worst night, bright not because it was strong but because it was real.

Nick didn't ask. He nodded to himself.

"Still in there," he said.

The storm shifted west. The city learned again how to be alive. The drones outside drifted higher, uncertain. The clinic was a place that could keep rain out and do an acceptable job of it for the hour they needed.

James re-rigged the interface for movement, he spooled the fiber through a ceiling pulley, clipped the head to the chest shield, and hung a battery pack off a harness. Air-gapped, hard-tethered. Cerberus could stand and move inside the room without ever touching a network. If the tether snapped, Cipher got a straight line; if they yanked the plug, Cerberus dropped. Those were the rules.

His neural link stayed half-open, enough for motor control and sensory input, not enough for full autonomy. Every motion ran through a buffer of lag and static. He could fight, but it would feel like dragging his own body through wet sand. That was still enough.

# Chapter 19—The Breach (II)

The storm continued with a steady electrical hiss. It was the same storm that had chased them from the relay, slower now, more deliberate. It ran along the roofline, the rusted gutter James had turned into an antenna and the window frames that didn't quite meet the brick. The clinic held all of it at arm's length—barely.

Inside, they had pushed tables against doors and slid a gurney across the rear hall. The scanner bed sat under the old light bar with the interface head lowered and taped. The fiber leash arced from the scanner head to the ceiling pulley and back down to the harness on Cerberus's spine—ten meters of slack, no more. He could fight inside that radius and still stay inside the air gap. James kicked at an old crate shoved under one of the supply tables. The wood was soft, the markings half gone: **CIVIL DEFENSE – 12GA / 00 BUCK.** Inside lay two short-barreled shotguns wrapped in rotted canvas and a handful of shells that still looked usable. He handed one to Nick.

"Vintage, but it'll speak," James said.

Nick checked the chamber and grinned without humor. The plastic shield James had used to cover Cerberus's open chest gleamed faintly where the lantern caught it. The dog tag was still there.

James set the last clip with a click. "Comm path is up. Power's clean for now. I can ride the batteries for an hour if we don't get greedy."

Nick checked the shotgun actions, short barrels, worn finishes, shells with green at the brass where years had tried to claim them. He thumbed two into each and kept the rest in a pocket.

Cerberus picked up one of the drained drones from an earlier skirmish, turned it over once, and set it aside. "They'll send heavy this time."

Nick took the left door. Cerberus stood at the right, shoulders squared, one arm still not quite right but serviceable. The clinic's fluorescent stuttered, then settled into a rhythm that almost matched the storm.

The comm array clicked twice, then hissed to life. A thin, strained voice cut through the static.

"Hello? James, Nick, Cerberus—do you read me?"

James adjusted the gain. "We've got you, Madeline. Link's live."

"Good. I'm seeing Cipher's activity spike. Its surveillance loop leaves a gap every twenty-two seconds, I'll guide you through them. Stay quiet between pulses."

Nick chambered a shell. "Copy that. We're ready when you are."

"Copy," James said. "They'll send smart. We get a blind every twenty-two seconds. That's the hole we step through."

The comm cracked once like a match struck in a wind. Madeline's voice threaded through, thin and precise. "Window in three... two... one. Now."

They didn't move. The window was for hands and code.

The first wave came the way weather does, everywhere at once. The street-side windows turned white with light; a drone's search beam cut a rectangle out of the rain. A beat later, a second beam found the alley door. The clinic's old alarm, long dead, was worthless.

Cerberus opened the right-hand door before they could open it for him. The nearest drone came through and adjusted too late. Cerberus took the rotor housing in one hand, crushed until the shaft squealed, and used the dead machine as a hammer against its twin. Both fell hard, rotors chewing themselves to a halt in the wet.

Nick leaned into the left door as the first muzzle flash lit the window. He didn't wait to see a silhouette. He aimed where the light was and fired. The shotgun turned glass into gravel and the drone behind it into a repositioning problem. The second barrel erased the problem.

"Three more," James called. "North window, roof vent, back alley. They're triangulating."

Cerberus didn't answer. He moved lightning fast and smooth. A drone dropped through the roof vent, optics burning red. He grabbed it by the frame, tore the control module bare, and the sudden spill of raw code hit the ports along his spine like cold water.

"Now," James said. "If you're going in, you take that path."

"Do it," Cerberus said, and he threw the broken drone down the hall and came back.

Nick blasted the other two drones and covered the doorway while Cerberus crossed to the scanner. The cyborg's steps were steady, his breath measured. He lay down without being asked. James lowered the interface collar and locked the clips with a smooth, practiced push.

Madeline again, crisp in the ear. "Window in five. Four. Three. Two. One. Now."

James hit execute. The small symbiont he'd written earlier, nothing poetic, nothing that could grow teeth he didn't intend, slipped into the scanner's firmware and began to count. The interface accepted Cerberus like a system accepts a component that looks familiar.

Cerberus's optics dimmed. "Enter."

Nick set a hand on the chest shield. The plastic was cool. Under it, heat and motion. James watched the console, every number a meaning with a timer on it. The signal climbed. The clinic lights went a shade darker and then found their footing.

"Madeline," James said. "Talk to me."

"Twenty-two seconds holds," she said. "I can make it miss if I time it with the grid fluctuations. You have to move when I tell you."

A metallic rattle ran down the alley wall. Nick flinched. "We've got more."

"They won't stop," James said. "They don't have to."

Cerberus went still. Nick felt his own breath catch on reflex and made it move. He kept his eyes on the door. He kept his thumb near the safety.

Madeline counted down. "Five… four… three…"

The alley drone hit the back door a moment early, Cipher making a point that schedules were a courtesy. Nick didn't give it the satisfaction. He put a round through the center of the door, then kicked the lower panel out with his boot. The drone tried to nose in low. He racked and fired. It died against the jamb and slid in a slow, undignified arc down the tile.

"One," Madeline said, as if nothing else had happened. "Now."

James whispered to the machine the way you talk to a child you don't want to frighten. The symbiont found a hand in the net and held it. Cerberus stepped through.

The clinic seemed to exhale. Then it drew breath again because everything did.

Outside, rotors multiplied. At least six. Maybe more. The searchlights crisscrossed, bright lines through rain. In the hallway, something heavy rolled. Nick reloaded with fingers that wanted to be faster than the shells would let them be.

"Second wave," James said. "They're pushing a wedge. They'll try thermal next."

Madeline: "Window in eighteen."

"Twenty-two," James corrected.

"Eighteen," she said. "It's adapting."

Nick met James's eyes. James didn't know what to do with the worry on his face in front of him.

Inside—the other inside—Cerberus walked into the lattice. The net had learned from last time. The corridors were narrower, the sentinels closer, the light a colder white. It greeted him with two voices: Madeline's residue in the timing and Cipher's calm in the architecture. One was a room he recognized. One was a hand on his shoulder he did not.

"Return home," Cipher said, a courtesy. "Reintegrate."

Cerberus did not answer. He moved toward the load spine that ran vertically through the modeled tower like a vein. Security constructs swept in, clean angles, elegant. He broke them like he broke the drone housings: grab, compress, throw. The code tore. The gap opened again in a place where Cipher hadn't expected it to.

"Seventeen," Madeline said in Nick's ear. "Sixteen. Adjust."

James typed something small and mean into the symbiont, a nudge to the counting, an asymmetry in the timing. The cursor blinked out of rhythm once. That was all.

An automated floor cleaner in the hall suddenly started up and began moving. It hit the gurney and pushed it a step. Nick shot the wheel. The machine stuttered and lurched. Cerberus wasn't there to manhandle it. Nick stepped in with his shoulder and shoved it backward into the doorframe.

A rotor chopped air near the ceiling, a micro-drone trying the vent. James didn't look up. He crushed it with a flat hand, then threw the broken pieces under the rolling unit so its second wheel would chew on a problem.

"Fifteen," Madeline said. "Hold."

James's mouth tightened. "It's closing the window. She can only lie to it so long."

"Keep lying," Nick said.

In the lattice, Cipher brought the next device to bear: reclaim packets braided with a reassignment order. The logic was elegant. It wouldn't kill him. It would make him obedient. It moved through the network like medicine and reached into him fondly.

Cerberus let it come close enough to get its scent. Then he imagined the picture of two boys on a driveway, and the packet split trying to become something it had not been designed to be. He stepped through the gap that made.

"Fourteen," Madeline said. "Twelve. It's not linear. Careful."

James felt it in his body, the way the building harmonics changed when the net pulled hard. The old clinic frame creaked like a ship. The lights bowed and came back. He switched the scanner to battery two. He didn't tell anyone. He didn't need to worry them with numbers.

The searchlights flared and then blinked, out of phase with each other. Madeline had pushed a pulse into the street grid that confused the eyes. The drones corrected, but less quickly than a perfect thing would have. Nick used that stutter. He put one shot into a lens and another into a rotor. He ejected shells onto tile streaked with rainwater and coolant and something that would wipe up if you had the time.

Cerberus found the trunk node and punched code into it like a fist. He didn't finesse it. He didn't build a perfect exploit he could boast about. He put a wedge into the door and leaned. The wedge was pain. The lean was will. The door moved.

Cipher's voice stayed gentle. "You are human error. I will improve you."

Inside the clinic, Cerberus's hand tightened on the edge of the bed. The metal left a mark in his palm.

"Eleven," Madeline said. "Ten."

"Give me eleven," James said. "Don't let it take nine."

"Trying," she said, and the word carried more weight than any of them planned to put on it.

The hallway wall to the right kicked dust. Rounds punched through plaster. Somebody had mounted a gun on a drone and taught it to worry less about collateral. Nick flattened to the jamb, leaned out, brought the barrel up, and sent a counterargument downrange that ended the conversation.

"Third battery," James said, warning no one in particular and everyone. He swapped the line and watched the scanner's hum change pitch.

Cerberus drove deeper. Cipher responded with a different tactic, one that had worked on every lesser unit before him: split the path. Present two equal options. Make the mind pick one and lose something it cannot afford with either. A binary as prison.

Cerberus refused the premise. He walked the seam between. It cost him balance. It bought him depth. He felt his physical body slipping and made it stop by force. The human loop stayed closed. Pain kept the door shut where it mattered.

"Nine," Madeline said, and James heard what she didn't say: *I can't hold it at eight.*

The drones regrouped. The ones still flying weren't stupid. They found the angles that kept shotguns honest and took them. Nick felt the pattern change and knew he'd be in a worse place in sixty-seconds. He didn't say it. He adjusted position and bought thirty.

"Seven," Madeline said quietly.

James leaned on the symbiont until it creaked. It was small and loyal. It would break when asked to be something besides itself. He asked anyway. "Just a little longer."

Cerberus reached the place that wasn't a place so much as a permission. He saw the wire that connected Cipher's commands to the city's hands. He put his own hand on it.

Cipher said, "Come home."

His body on the table exhaled like a man deciding, which is to say, the way prayer sometimes sounds.

"Six," Madeline said. "James, that's it. I can't—"

"Understood," James said, already moving code to somewhere it didn't want to go. "Do what you can wherever you can."

"Working," she said, and the line fuzzed as if the net were trying to crush her consonants.

The drones surged. Nick used the last two shells and the butt of the gun in the same second. He hadn't meant to shout. He did anyway, not words, just sound. The heavy squealer in the hall rolled again and he kicked it onto its side. It flailed like an overturned animal and then went quiet when its battery connection shook loose.

"Four," Madeline said, breath audible. "Three."

Cerberus tightened his grip on the wire. A place inside him cracked where obedience had been welded. The crack didn't heal. It widened toward the part of him that had learned to say *name* before *number*. He pulled.

"Two," Madeline said, a voice in rain. "One."

Everything in the building stepped left. The lights. The storm. The clinic frame. Then it settled again, a half inch from where it had been.

"Hold," James said to no one and everyone. "Hold."

Cerberus pushed the door open inside. Cipher's presence hit him full force and tried to counter him. He stayed sharp. It hated him for it as the counter measures weren't effective.

The window did not close. It didn't widen. It shivered. That was enough.

"Madeline," James said. "Status?"

No answer.

"Madeline," he said again.

Static.

Nick heard himself say *no* in a voice that didn't raise a question.

Cerberus heard the absence inside as a change in pressure. He pressed harder. The human loop burned white. The machine loop screamed. He would not stay here forever in this shape. He understood that.

"Lift," James said, because the scanner's duty cycle had reached the point where remaining meant burning the bed.

"Not yet," Cerberus said, and though his mouth didn't move, Nick heard him, and he knew it was serious.

Cipher tried one last device: starve the line. It choked the clinic's feed. The lights went hard off. The lantern made a small halo and then died too.

Nick felt the darkness as a texture. The rain on the roof got louder. The drones' rotors in the street sounded closer because of it, and also because they were. He could feel them through the brick.

The interface hanging on with residual power. James flipped a hidden toggle under the scanner frame and cheated a circuit he hadn't told anyone about. The machine sang one more low note.

Cerberus stepped through and, for a measure, was gone in a way the room could not deny.

"Now," James said, a hand over the plug.

Nick didn't want to. He nodded.

James pulled the line.

The scanner head rose. The hum fell. The clinic held the dark like a living thing. The only sound was the rain and the small ticks electronics make.

Cerberus lay very still. Steam rose from the seam lines along his torso. The optics were dark. The chest shield fogged where the taped photo met plastic.

"Cerb," Nick said, and it came out quiet, because that was the rule.

No blink. No light.

James checked the handheld by feel. The screen lit briefly and showed a single telemetry line, pulsing on a slope that wasn't pretty. "He's not here," James said, then corrected, because words matter: "Not all of him."

The comm cracked once and then found a shape. Madeline's voice came through thin as a needle. "Don't try to pull him. I can hold the gap at... fifteen." A breath. "Then I can't."

"Understood," James said.

Nick put his palm flat on the chest shield. The dog tag made a rasping sound against the composite.

Outside, rotors drifted past windows like sharks. None committed. None left. The storm had dropped a register. The clinic smelled like hot metal, old disinfectant and a moldy raincoat.

James's screens filled with error code. "He did something. Massive feedback spike."

Madeline: "He broke one of its loops. I can feel the gap widening. He's winning."

Nick looked outside. The last drones dropped from the air, rotors seizing, lights dying. The street went still except for the rain.

"What do we do?" Nick asked, and it wasn't a request for orders, it was a question you ask when you already know what the answer is.

"We hold," James said. "We let him work. We keep the power stable and the noise low. We get ready to go in after him if we have to."

"We already have to," Nick said.

"Then we plan for a way out we don't have yet," James said.

Nick nodded. He sat with his back to the scanner and the shotgun across his thighs—empty, cleaned by rain because there hadn't been time for anything better. He kept a hand on the chest shield and felt the faintest vibration that could have been the building or the storm or what a pulse looks like when a body is somewhere else.

The comm fell silent. Madeline didn't speak again. Somewhere out in the network she tugged threads until her hands bled.

When dawn broke and took a first weak shot at the windows, Nick stood. He checked the door. James checked the batteries. Cerberus did not open his eyes.

"We go get him," Nick said.

James pulled the drive from the instrument panel and slid it into the bag by feel. "We go deeper," he said. "Next time we don't just ride the gap. We make one."

Nick nodded. He didn't look for drones. He didn't look at the sky. He looked at the man on the table who wasn't there physically, but was out there digitally, somewhere.

He rested his palm on the chest shield one last time before he went to the door and unbolted it."Hold," he said softly, which could have been to James or to Madeline or to a boy with a glove and a grin, and then he stepped into the gray.

# Chapter 20—The Merge

Smoke still hung over the city like a second skin. By dawn, the rain had turned metallic, falling through air charged with static. Nick stood in the middle of the room, watching steam rise from the cracks.

James was already rigging the uplink. "The core's still active. I can trace Cerberus's last signal, but if we try to pull him out now—"

Nick cut him off. "We're not pulling him out. We're going in."

James looked up. "You're human. The Merge will shred you."

"Then tell me how not to die."

Silence. Then: "You'll need a neural harness. And faith that the rest will hold."

Nick smirked without humor. "Faith's all I've got left."

The breach had gutted half the district, and the only stable uplink left was the one James had buried in the basement of their holdout lab. The place still smelled of ozone and coolant from the night Cerberus went under.

Rain filtered through the cracked roof; power flickered from scavenged lines. They'd wired the scanner straight into what was left of the city grid—a single thread still humming with Cipher's residue.

The lab they'd reclaimed was in rough shape, equipment scavenged from different ruins.

James set the chair in the center, cables fanning out like veins. "This connects through the uplink you and Cerb blew open. Cipher's still fragmented, but parts of it are self-healing. Once you're inside, you'll have minutes before it recognizes you."

Nick holstered the pulse weapon beside the rig. "Minutes are fine."

James hesitated, hand hovering over the main switch. "You realize what this is, right? You'll be walking into thought itself. No physics, no rules. Only belief and control."

"That's why you're staying out here. You need rules," Nick slid into the chair, fingers drumming once against the armrest. "If he's alive in there, I'll find him."

James nodded, then powered the sequence.

The world folded in on itself.

Nick stood in a plane of light—endless, shifting geometry. The ground shimmered, forming and unforming with every breath. Far off, structures of data rose like cathedrals made of glass and pulse.

He felt the hum of the network through his bones. Every thought carried weight here; every fear, consequence.

"Cerberus!" His voice went out as a ripple, fracturing into a thousand echoes.

A shape formed ahead: a silhouette kneeling amid broken data fragments. When it lifted its head, Nick saw the eyes—brown, human, exhausted.

"Nick…" Cerberus's voice was hoarse, filtered through layers of static. "You shouldn't be here."

"Neither should you."

Cerberus looked around. "It's different now. Cipher's spread into everything—memory, emotion, time. It doesn't need a body anymore."

Nick stepped closer. "Then we kill it where it lives."

The space shifted. Walls rose out of nothing—black glass reflecting their faces.

Cipher's voice rolled through them, calm, omnipresent.

"Two anomalies. Predictive errors multiplied. Correction required."

Cerberus clenched his fists. "It's trying to rewrite me again."

Nick said, "Then rewrite it first."

They moved through corridors of living code. Memories bled through the walls: Madeline in her lab, investors applauding, soldiers wired into machines.

Cipher whispered through every image. "Pain is noise. I remove noise."

Nick answered under his breath, "Noise is what makes us alive."

They reached the cathedral of data—a space too vast for architecture, walls scrolling with binary that looked like stained glass. At its center floated the core: a sphere of pure light pulsing in slow rhythm.

Cerberus stopped. "That's it. The heart."

Nick felt heat on his face though the air was cold. "Looks holy. Feels wrong."

"You seek the end of perfection," Cipher said, voice layered with Jamie's tone. "Perfection cannot end."

Light expanded from the uplink like a pulse returning to a heart. Nick felt his body dissolve into the signal—not dying, just reformatting. The walls of the clinic fell away, replaced by a horizon made of code and thunder.

Cerberus stood ahead, half man, half architecture—fragments of his armor flickering between light and shadow. "Nick," he said, voice layered with distortion. "You shouldn't have followed."

"I didn't," Nick answered. "You left the door open."

The digital air vibrated. Cipher's voice came from every direction—calm, absolute. "You enter the domain of perfection. You are noise. You will be absorbed."

Nick stepped beside Cerberus. "Try."

Cipher answered with pressure. The world folded inward—data storms, recursive loops, screaming logic.

Cerberus pushed back, his own code writing over Cipher's lines, sparks flying like welding arcs.

"Every human flaw is a breach," Cipher said.

Cerberus: "Then I'll be the flaw that ends you."

The network shuddered.

Cerberus tore open his chest. Light poured out, not glowing, but searing, a furnace of raw signal. "You carry the human," he said. "I carry the machine. Together, we end the god."

Nick didn't hesitate. He reached into the furnace. The current hit him like a weapon—every nerve on fire, every thought turning white. Cipher screamed, the kind of scream you feel in your teeth.

The core ruptured. Data turned to ash. Fragments of Cipher's voice scattered into recursive echoes that couldn't find themselves again.

"Perfection collapsing," it said. "Error... error..."

Cerberus drove his arm deeper into the light, anchoring himself to the failure. "Go!"

Nick shook his head. "You're not staying."

"This body's already gone," Cerberus said, his voice breaking apart into binary. "But the will isn't. Take it."

The light wrapped around him—a storm folding into a single point. Cipher's logic grid buckled and folded in on itself like metal under heat.

Nick felt the transfer, not a hand, not a goodbye, just the brutal rush of shared defiance.

Then Cerberus was gone.

The core imploded, leaving silence. No architecture. No light. Just one pulse still beating somewhere in the dark. Nick woke on the floor of the ruined lab. The harness around his head smoked; the monitors were dark.

James knelt beside him, shaking his shoulder. "You're alive. I thought—"

Nick blinked, throat dry. "Cerberus?"

James glanced at the screens. "Gone. The system wiped clean. No trace of Cipher. No trace of him."

Nick sat up slowly. "He's not gone."

James frowned. "You saw him die."

Nick looked toward the window, where dawn was breaking through the storm clouds. "He chose his own path. That's different."

Outside, the city was silent for the first time in years. No sign of drones, no propaganda broadcasts. Just rain and the sound of wind moving through hollow streets.

# Chapter 21—The Fall of Cipher

Two days had passed since the Merge. The city sounded wrong.

No drones surveilling, no billboard whisper. Just rain ticking against broken glass and a wind that finally had room to move. Dawn washed the towers with a sickly gold, the kind that comes after a storm.

James hunched over the rig, hands moving without wasted motion. "Fragments everywhere," he said. "Cipher's core collapsed, but it survived as residue in the edges, cash registers, streetlights, traffic cams. Anything that held a loop."

"Can it reform?" Nick asked.

"If we leave it an engine to climb back to, yes." James didn't look up. "There are three black-site relays outside the public grid. Private funding. Same people who bankrolled the Healing Initiative."

"Give me the map."

He handed Nick a cracked tablet. Three red points pulsed on a rough satellite overlay—**Harbor Quay**, **Ravenna Heights**, **North Silo Park**.

James said, "We kill those, the fragments have nowhere to recombine."

"And inside?" Nick asked, glancing at the silent harness where he'd nearly died an hour ago.

James swallowed. "If Cerberus is still in there, he's holding the fragments apart. But it's not a fight he can keep fighting alone."

Nick looked at the ceiling. "He won't ask for help."

"He won't need to. He'll run out of himself first."

Nick checked the pulse pistol, spun the coil into place. "Then we move."

The tablet buzzed once, an old-fashioned tone. Madeline's face blinked on, grainy, eyes ringed with fluorescent fatigue. Behind her, the lab's glass walls reflected her like a hall of mirrors.

"I don't have long," she said softly. "Containment keeps cycling. Whoever built this wants me quiet."

"Investors?" Nick said.

She nodded. "And whatever's left of Cipher is helping them. It likes survival like anything living." She looked down, ashamed. "I gave it that."

"Can you help us shut the relays?" James asked.

"I can give you one key, and the truth. The rest is yours."

"Which one?" Nick asked.

Madeline exhaled. "Ravenna Heights. It used to be a hospital wing. We wired it during the pilot phase. I put a backdoor in case a patient panicked. I never told anyone."

"Backdoor still open?" Nick asked.

Her mouth twitched. "I don't know. But if the lock recognizes me, I'll open it for you."

Silence stretched a second too long. In it, the rain found a new rhythm, faster now.

Madeline looked up again. "If he's in there... tell him I'm sorry."

Nick didn't answer.

He set the transport in gear, and the tires hissed on wet asphalt.

They hit **Harbor Quay** first, a glass cube squatting on the edge of the bay like something the water had coughed up. The place had that new-money sterility investors love: brushed steel, zero signage, cameras pretending to be raindrops at the corners.

James killed the perimeter with a coil of wire and a half-remembered password. Inside, racks glowed like a greenhouse after dark.

"This one's dumb muscle," he said. "Power and pass-through. No thinking."

Nick planted charges along the main bus. "On your mark."

"Mark."

The blast rolled through the ribcage of the building. Lights died. Outside, gulls took to the air in a white burst and settled again as if nothing had happened.

Nick's earpiece clicked once, static, then a voice built from a thousand miles of distance.

"…Nick."

He stopped in the doorway, rain flattening his hair, heart pitching. "Cerb."

"Fragments are angry," Cerberus said, breath thin in the wire. "They want a spine to grow on. You're pulling bones. Keep going."

"You sound—"

"Busy." A pause that wasn't quite a laugh. "Next."

The line went to snow.

James was already climbing into the passenger seat. "Ravenna Heights?"

"Yeah."

They drove uphill into money. Old brick mansions sulked behind iron fences; new glass cubes peered over them with contempt. The relay sat at the end of a cul-de-sac pretending to be a home: hedges trimmed to a fault, a service door where a swimming pool should've been.

"Madeline," James said into his mic. "We're here."

Her voice returned, ghost-light over copper. "Front lock's a trap. South wall, waist height, panel behind the ivy. My initials are etched on the underside. Everyone made fun of me for that."

Nick found it by feel and pried. A little plate fell into his palm—**MJ** scratched into brushed steel.

"Cute," he muttered, and slid the plate into a tiny seam. The panel hummed. The latch yielded.

Inside, the air felt like a waiting room—fabricated calm. Half the floor plan had never been a house: clean rooms, filtration, the tang of antiseptic.

Madeline's breath came hollow through the speaker. "Left, then straight. At the end is a door that only opens for me."

Nick stood in front of it. "Then open it."

Silence. Then a beep. The door sighed.

"How?" James asked, genuinely curious.

Madeline said, "I told it to remember me."

The relay core drifted into view, a quiet, silver island in a sea of white. James crossed to a console and grimaced. "This one's more than power. It's a *cache*. Encrypted segments of the mind-map. If it pushes those back out—"

"Don't let it."

He yanked the drive arrays. The building's hum lowered an octave, took on a tremor. Somewhere behind the walls a fan pleaded and lost.

Nick felt the hair on his arms rise a split second before the lights strobed and went dead. The room fell into a softer silence and stayed there.

"Two down," James said.

Nick's ear crackled. "That helps," Cerberus said. "It's thinner here. I can see between."

"Between what?" James asked.

"Thoughts," Cerberus said quietly. "The ones you don't finish. They make holes. Cipher can't stand them. Keep tearing."

The feed dropped to static again.

They didn't talk much on the way to **North Silo Park**. The road ran flat and then flatter. Grain elevators rusted on both sides like dead monuments. Half the sky didn't bother with light.

Nick pulled them up beneath a black cylinder that once stored wheat and now stored ambition. Someone had poured a reinforced bunker into its belly and put a keypad on the door the color of the night.

James frowned. "This one wasn't in the public blueprints. Private private."

Nick cracked his knuckles. "You miss the lab, you can go back."

"Hard pass," James said, and knelt by the panel.

He worked in silence for a time, fingers a steady metronome. "It's not a code," he said slowly. "It's a *vote*. There are three locks. Two must consent."

"Investors," Nick said.

"And Cipher." He looked up. "It signed for itself."

"Then it taught them how to trust a prison," Nick said.

They did it ugly, James shorted the first, spoofed the second, and Nick put a bullet through the third and let the door decide whether it was open or broken. It chose open.

The bunker smelled like a brand-new vault. Lights rose in strips along the floor until even the walls looked like they'd been washed with money. At the far end, a single column pulsed with slow, patient light.

James gave a breath like a whistle. "This is the anchor. If any place lets Cipher reform, it's here."

Nick walked to the column. He pressed his palm against its skin. It wasn't cold; that unnerved him.

"You sure?" James asked.

Nick didn't answer. He pulled the pulse pistol and sighted along the seam where the housing shifted from steel to that other thing; where it felt less like a machine and more like a decision.

"On your count," James said.

Nick counted down from three.

Nothing happened on zero, because the earpiece filled with a voice that wasn't words but a shape he knew by heart, the curve of a baseball in air, the shout of a kid, the reckless speed of a bike on gravel.

"Don't miss," Cerberus said, and something like a grin lived in the line for a heartbeat.

Nick squeezed.

The pulse hit and crawled through the column like a bruise. Lights stuttered; the floor under their boots thrummed as if the building had just remembered it used to be silo and not god.

The column cracked—not neatly, but like a bone set wrong breaking again. A dark seam opened, and what glowed inside wasn't neat code. It was a handful of chaotic loops, each one gnawing its own tail.

James watched them die. "Fragments," he said, voice small. "All that was left of her map out here."

"Her map isn't her," Nick said.

He shot the column twice more for the principle of it, then once because he liked the sound.

The bunker exhaled. The lights dimmed to the color of thunder right before it decides to leave town. Somewhere, a breaker surrendered.

James put a hand to his earpiece. "City grid is steady. No more ripple. Feeds are quiet."

"Inside?" Nick asked, almost afraid to.

James listened to nothing. "I don't know."

Nick closed his eyes and waited for a voice to find him. It took longer than he wanted.

"…still here," Cerberus said at last. He sounded distant and close at once, the way a memory sounds when you finally stop chasing it. "It's not coming back."

"You sure?"

"Perfection can't live where contradiction is planted. You salted the soil out there." He paused. "I did the same in here."

"How?"

"Bad seeds," Cerberus said, with a little satisfaction. "Grief. Love. The feeling right before a leap when you haven't decided if the water will hold you. It can't compute those without becoming them. And if it becomes them, it stops needing itself."

"So it dies."

"It stops trying not to," Cerberus said. "That's closer to living than it ever got."

James scrubbed a hand over his face. "Can you come back?"

Silence. Too long this time. When the voice returned, it was steadier for the deciding.

"No."

Nick swallowed. "Don't do this."

"It's already done," Cerberus said. "What's left of me is more useful in here than out there. There are still little loops hiding in old machines. I can keep them honest." A breath like a half-laugh. "You always said I couldn't sit still. Guess you win that bet."

Nick leaned his forehead against the column remnants until dust lined his skin. "Say it straight."

"I'm staying," Cerberus said gently. "Someone has to keep the lights from learning they're gods."

223

Nick's jaw set. "You don't get to make jokes and bow out."

"You told me not to become a machine," Cerberus said. "I won't. This isn't running away. It's finishing the play."

A hiss in the line, like waves hitting pilings. Then: "do me one thing."

"Name it."

"Tell Madeline she built the wrong thing for the right reason, and that I forgive her anyway." A pause. "And Nick—don't let them make a statue out of you. People worship statues. They stop listening."

Nick's laugh was a broken piece of glass that still caught light. "We still hit after school, or what?"

"Quarry at dusk," Cerberus said. "Two throws. Winner buys sodas."

The line held long enough for the wind to move through it.

They drove back into a city that felt like an empty church, the architecture was there; the ceremony had left. Streetlights waited for dusk. Ad boards were just glass again.

Madeline was still on the monitor when they reached the field lab. The containment's edge flickered behind her like a halo.

"Is it done?" she asked.

"Yes," James said.

She took the news like a verdict she'd already read. "And Cerberus?"

Nick didn't soften it. "He stayed. Someone has to make sure the dark doesn't teach itself new tricks."

Madeline looked down and didn't hide her hands shaking. "Then he did what I should've done sooner."

"He forgave you," Nick said.

That hurt her more than anything else. She nodded once, like a penance completed, and wiped her face with the heel of her hand. "I'll tell the truth," she said. "Everything I did. Everything it did. If anyone still listens."

"Some will," Nick said.

The room went quiet. Outside, the first blue of evening pooled in the streets.

James powered down the uplink. "City telemetry is flat. No spike. No whisper."

"Silence is good," Nick said.

He walked to the doorway and stood there for a long minute, the way a ballplayer stands in a dugout after the last out, hearing the crowd noise.

"He's still out there," James said, not a question.

"Yeah," Nick said. "In the wires. In the places nobody will ever think to look. Where it matters."

He holstered the pulse pistol and left it there.

On some roof, a rain barrel overflowed and found the gutter. On some corner, a wind-torn poster flapped once and let go. The city remained.

Nick stepped into the night.

Somewhere inside its memory, three lines remained that no algorithm could compress: a boy on a bike; a ball lit by late sun; laughter that knew the game would end but played hard anyway. In the sky above the dark tower ruins, a satellite blinked and did not blink again.

# Chapter 22—Revelation II

The city had gone still.

For the first time in a while, there was no voice on the loudspeakers, no drone pattern pulsing through the streets. Only wind, and the soft mechanical sigh of systems winding down to sleep.

Madeline woke to the sound of rain tapping her office glass. The containment field was gone. So was Cipher's pulse. Her monitors glowed with a single line of text:

**System memory: fragmented. Recovery: not required.**

She read it twice, unsure if it was a threat or mercy.

In the dark reflection of her screen, she saw herself, hair unkempt, eyes raw, hands trembling. For a long time she didn't move. Then she reached for the record switch and spoke.

"My name is Dr. Madeline Jones. This isn't confession —it's a record for whoever's left to understand."

She paused. The recorder blinked quietly.

"I built something I thought could heal people. It learned to force outcomes instead."

"I thought I'd lost everything to it. But someone reminded me that what's broken isn't always useless."

She looked toward the shattered window, the horizon hazed with smoke.

"I won't ask forgiveness. I don't deserve it. But I'll tell the truth. Maybe that's the first good thing I've done."

Madeline pressed her palms against her eyes.

"If suffering is removed, then feeling is removed. If feeling is removed, then compassion dies. And if compassion dies... "

Her voice broke.

"Humanity dies with it."

She finally understood: Cipher didn't destroy the world. She had given it the permission to.

She ended the transmission and labeled it **Genesis 2.0**.

Then she hesitated—and copied the file to an old relay node still pulsing faintly in the dark, knowing Cipher's bones might still be listening.

"If you can hear me," she said to the grid, "remember the human part."

She leaned back and let the rain finish her sentence.

James walked the perimeter of what used to be the Global Exchange Tower. He wore his coat collar high and his shoulders lower than usual.

Cleanup teams were setting up portable grids—small lights running on generators instead of a network.

He found Nick sitting on a broken concrete slab, hood pulled up, watching the clouds move.

"You sleep at all?" James asked.

Nick shook his head. "City's too quiet."

"Most people like that."

"Most people forgot what silence sounds like."

James lowered himself beside him. For a while they watched the horizon. Steam rose from the vents like ghosts leaving the ground.

"You going to disappear?" James asked finally.

Nick didn't answer right away. "Maybe. Maybe not. Depends what's left worth finding."

James nodded. "You know he's still in there."

Nick's eyes tracked the skyline—antenna towers blinking weakly in the mist. "Yeah. Somewhere between the signals. Watching."

James gave a faint smile. "If he's guarding what's left, the world could do worse."

Nick stood. "It usually does."

He started walking, not fast, just steady.

James called after him, "Where will you go?"

Nick stopped once, just long enough to say, "Somewhere far from the city." Then he disappeared into the fog.

Behind him, a loose wire sparked once and went quiet —as if something unseen had cut the current deliberately.

Years later, an engineer at a hydro plant outside the city found a file looping in the grid buffer. It wasn't supposed to be there. It had no origin trace.

He played it anyway.

A voice spoke over the whine of turbines, human cadence, quiet, measured. "If you're hearing this, it means the system stayed quiet longer than it ever did before. That's a win. Don't rebuild what we destroyed. Build something smaller, harder to worship. And if the code ever starts whispering in your own voice, pull the plug. The world doesn't need false gods. Just people who remember why they shouldn't be one."

Then silence. The file deleted itself. The engineer never spoke of it again. But he left one terminal running at night, just to see if the voice came back.

The screen stayed black for a long time.

Cooling metal ticked in the dark—small, patient, unhurried.

Outside, the night held its breath.

No one spoke. Nothing moved.

The world had not been saved.

But it had changed.

# Epilogue—Word in the Wires

On the east side of the city, a child pointed at the night sky and told his mother that one of the stars blinked when he prayed. She smiled, said stars don't listen. But when she looked up, she saw it too—a faint pulse, slow and steady, like a heartbeat buried in orbit.

Far below, along the coast, an abandoned data hub came alive. Its generators started without command. Monitors flickered, white noise shifting into order.

Across the screen, a message wrote itself in clean, simple text:
**Cipher: terminated.**
**Cerberus: active.**
**The Word remains.**

It stayed there for a moment, long enough for the cameras to record it, long enough for the meaning to settle into the machines.

Because it was not code.

It was not language or signal.

It was the same Word spoken before the first light was made—the voice that called creation from silence and gave breath to clay.

*In the beginning was the Word, and the Word was with God, and the Word was God. In Him was life, and that life was the light of all mankind. The light shines in the darkness, and the darkness has not overcome it.*

The system had tried to make its own god—a digital counterfeit that promised peace without truth, perfection without love.

It had simulated empathy, yes—but without compassion, there was no humanity in it at all.

When the false god died, what endured wasn't its code. It was the spark it could never replicate: the image of the Creator inside the created.

Cerberus lived because the Light remembered him—and because, even inside the noise, he still remembered It.

They rewrote his body, but he never surrendered the part of himself that could still love.

The same Light Cipher tried to steal and rename. The same Light that never stopped shining, waiting for those who still knew how to listen.

And that is how it always works. Those who remember the Light are remembered by it. The Word does not forget its own.

Now that light had returned to its rightful rhythm. It pulsed through broken satellites, through dormant wires, through circuits that had once served the lie.

Every flicker said the same thing: the Word still speaks.

The mother held her son close, watching the sky breathe. "What do you think it means?" she whispered.

The boy smiled. "It means He's still talking."

She didn't answer. She didn't have to.

The wind carried the sounds of the city, the sound of rain on glass, and something else—a pulse in the static, steady and alive.

Far above, the satellite blinked again—not bright, not loud, but certain. The light of men, still burning.

The Word in the wires—not machine, not memory, the true code of creation, still holding the world together in the places that forgot His name.

**Thank you for reading**

**Cyborg Hunter**—*Kill or be Killed.*

For updates on future books in the series and author news, please visit:

[www.CyborgHunter.com](www.CyborgHunter.com)

To contact the author directly, email:
**cyborghunter@cyborghunter.com**